Taking hold of  **brought her in f... he'd made to co... desert night crac... the moon beamed down benevolently. Everything was as it should be, but he still got the feeling that everything in his rigidly controlled life was about to change.**

"I think you'd rather be with me, in the tent," Isla whispered.

"Have you learned nothing?" he demanded, putting her away from him. Impatiently, he toed the cushions into place.

As she reached for him, it became clear that she had not. And this time he'd call her bluff.

The air between them was electric as Shazim drew her deeper into his erotic net. Closing her eyes, she inhaled deeply and shakily as he dipped his head to lightly brush her lips with his. His kiss was like a question: Did she want to carry on? Her answer was yes, most certainly. This time she reached up and laced her fingers through his hair to keep him close. Her senses were full of him. He intoxicated her. He tasted of all things good. He smelled of wood smoke and sandalwood, and the delicate balance between her fear of physical love and the growing sense that she was safe with him reached tipping point. Realistically, she was in the greatest danger of her life. Shazim's destiny called him to greater things than a girl by a campfire in the desert. But she had no intention of spending the rest of her life wondering what a night with Shazim would be like.

Dear Reader,

It's hard to believe this is my fiftieth romance. I dreamed of writing one. I struggled to write one. My first book took me eighteen months to write. Honing my craft to the point where my story was ready took me two years—probably longer.

Books and stories provide friends to believe in, and an introduction to many different, exciting worlds. At school, essay writing was the lesson I looked forward to more than any other as I anticipated the moment when I would be able to share my dreams. When I began to write in earnest, I collected a box of rejections—and threw them out, thinking I was finished with dreaming. How wrong could I be! The last rejection was from an editor at Harlequin, but they asked if I had anything else. It took a friend to point out, "What could you lose by submitting one more story?"

One thing I learned—one thing I can pass on to you, is *never give up*. It doesn't matter what you're striving for—keep at it. Learn from everything you get wrong, and put right what you can, then forge ahead. That last push might be the one that gets you where you want to be—though that's when the hard work starts!

Writing is amazing, though frustrating at times, but the reward of friendship across the world— from readers, fellow authors and other publishing professionals, have been a blessing I could never have anticipated.

Thank you all for everything you give to me.

Susan

Susan Stephens

IN THE SHEIKH'S SERVICE

Recycling programs
for this product may
not exist in your area.

ISBN-13: 978-0-373-13938-5

In the Sheikh's Service

First North American Publication 2016

Copyright © 2016 by Susan Stephens

Printed in U.S.A.

HARLEQUIN®
www.Harlequin.com

Susan Stephens was a professional singer before meeting her husband on the Mediterranean island of Malta. In true Harlequin Presents style they met on Monday, became engaged on Friday and married three months later. Susan enjoys entertaining, travel and going to the theater. To relax she reads, cooks and plays the piano, and when she's had enough of relaxing she throws herself off mountains on skis, or gallops through the countryside singing loudly.

Books by Susan Stephens

Harlequin Presents

Bound to the Tuscan Billionaire
Master of the Desert

Hot Brazilian Nights!

In the Brazilian's Debt
At the Brazilian's Command
Brazilian's Nine Months' Notice
Back in the Brazilian's Bed

The Skavanga Diamonds

Diamond in the Desert
The Flaw in His Diamond
The Purest of Diamonds?
His Forbidden Diamond

The Acostas!

The Untamed Argentinian
The Shameless Life of Ruiz Acosta
The Argentinian's Solace
A Taste of the Untamed
The Man from Her Wayward Past
Taming the Last Acosta

Visit the Author Profile page at Harlequin.com for more titles.

Thanks to the late Penny Jordan,
and to Lucy Mukerjee, my first editor
at Harlequin, for believing in me.

CHAPTER ONE

A POLE-DANCING CLUB across from the Michelin-starred restaurant where he was dining with his ambassador was an unhappy coincidence. He should have known what to expect when his people booked the ambassador's favourite table for dinner. This was Soho, London, England, where strip clubs coexisted happily with top-end eateries, but the ambassador was an old friend, and Shazim had fallen in with the old man's wish to try something new. The downside was that the ambassador's son had come along too.

Sitting still seemed beyond the edgy thirty-something. Girls dancing in the club across the road had grabbed his attention. It wasn't just the guy's blatant lack of good manners Shazim found appalling, but something more nagging at his senses. Whatever happened, he would not allow the ambassador's son to harass the girls.

'Have you finished eating?' The ambassador's

son stared imploringly at him. 'Can we look in across the road?'

He was like a puppy on a leash. Shazim had to grab a glass to steady it as he lurched away from the table in his hurry to leave the restaurant.

Shazim caught up with him at the door. His security guys hovered. With a look, he ordered his men to stand down.

'Aren't you a bit old for this?' He angled his chin towards the rose-tinted windows of the club, where shadowy forms were undulating back and forth.

By this time the ambassador had joined them, and there was real danger of a scene. 'Go with him, Shazim,' the ambassador begged. 'See that he doesn't get into trouble, will you? Please? For me?'

Tasking one of his team to escort the elder statesman home, he thrust a bundle of notes into the maître d's hand and followed the ambassador's son out of the restaurant.

Oh, for goodness' sake! This was ridiculous. Her friend Chrissie wasn't exactly lacking in the bosom department, but Chrissie wasn't exactly overabundant, either, Isla fretted as she attempted to squeeze her ample frontage into the microscopic bikini top.

If someone had asked Isla to name the very

last thing on earth she liked to do, it would be to make herself look provocative in front of a room full of men—and there was every reason for that, but Chrissie was a good friend and Chrissie had a family emergency tonight.

The past couldn't reach out and hurt her, Isla told herself firmly, not unless she allowed it to, and tonight it wouldn't.

Her mother's death eighteen months ago had left her shaken to the core, and what had happened directly after the funeral could still send her reeling, but tonight was Chrissie's night, so she would get on with the job—if she could force her breasts into submission. Turning this way and that, she measured the risk factor of her breasts going one way while she went the other. Here was living proof that no one could squeeze a quart into a pint pot. Nor could they make a plain, stocky woman into a sugarplum fairy overnight. She was a down-to-earth mature student in the veterinary sciences department. Far from being the glamorous type, she usually had grime of unspeakable origins beneath her fingernails. On the plus side, the costume was gorgeous. She loved a bit of twinkle, and the bikini was a deep, rich pink, exquisitely decorated with glittering crystal beads and sequins. It would look fantastic on Chrissie, as it would on any woman with a normal figure, but on Isla's super-sized, top-heavy figure?

It looked like a sparkling bandage wrapped around a bun.

One of the many jobs Isla had taken in order to pay her fees at the university was to lead a class of enthusiastic children in gymnastics at the university gym, but she wore a sports bra for that, not an unfit-for-purpose sequinned bikini. This was the first time she could remember having a flexible body and the ability to use it being both an advantage and a disadvantage. She would never have agreed to do this if Chrissie's need hadn't been greater than Isla's fear of ever making it seem that she was trying to lead a man on. Once upon an ugly time, that accusation had been cruelly levelled at her, and it had left a lingering doubt.

She had to hope the apprehension she was feeling went away once she lost herself in practising her moves for the Christmas concert at the gym.

Get over yourself and get out there—

She swung around at a knock on the door.

'Five minutes, please,' a disembodied male voice informed her.

Five minutes? She'd need five hours to make this disaster fly! She took a last look in the mirror and wished her breasts would shrink.

'I'll be there,' she called out, slipping on her

high-heeled shoes with agitated fingers. She'd kick the heels off once she got started, but Chrissie had said first impressions were all-important to the audience, and she had no intention of letting Chrissie down.

There were certain things that came with ruling a country Shazim could do without. Tolerating the offspring of loyal subjects was one of them. Entering a pole-dancing club in order to prevent the ambassador's son hitting on one of the girls was another. Most clubs ran a strict 'no-touch' policy, but the ambassador's spawn was the type to do as he pleased and then hide behind diplomatic immunity.

As he negotiated the mass of men in the overheated club, he thought about his elder brother, and the strength it had taken him to wear the yoke of duty. There were a lot of things about being a king that held no appeal.

Shazim had not been trained to be a king, but the tragedy in the desert, for which he held himself responsible, had thrust him into the role, opening his eyes to a burden his brother had carried so lightly. Following his brother's death, Shazim, the reckless brother, had become poacher turned gamekeeper, and there was no way he would allow shame to fall on his people's heads because of the ambassador's son.

'Can I get you something, sir?'

He eyed the girl. Beautiful. Slender. But with a wary gaze beneath her glossy shell. 'No. Nothing. Thank you.' Removing the ambassador's son from the club with the minimum of fuss was his only goal.

'A seat, sir?'

He glanced at the second girl. Her eyes were as dead as those of the girl currently working the pole. 'No, thank you.' He continued to hone in on his target.

His work in London was crucial, and he would not allow some brash, overindulged diplomat's son to get in the way of it by attracting adverse publicity. Creating a nature reserve where endangered species could breed safely in their natural habitat required specialist knowledge, and he had found all he could need at the nearby university where he was investing millions in research and new buildings in order to bring his late brother's dream to reality.

Waving his security team away, he took the ambassador's son by the arm. The man resisted him with a violent shake and a lot of cursing, but then, realising who he was swearing at, he went limp and began to stutter some excuse that Shazim had no interest in hearing. Ushering him away with a not so subtle warning, he sent him back to daddy with a flea in his ear.

He had intended to follow the ambassador's son out of the club when something made him stop and look around at the stage where another girl was about to start dancing. She was different from the rest, if only because she was smiling. He felt irritated on her behalf when the man next to him commented, 'She's sensational. What a rack—'

There was no denying that the girl was attractive. She was full figured and proud of it. Her skin was honey pale and as smooth as silk, but it was her happy face that held him. She seemed lost in thought, but her uplifting aura was enough to hold every man in the club transfixed as she worked her body enthusiastically on the pole.

Leaning back against a pillar, he stayed to watch. She was skilful and sexy, with both flair and talent, but there was nothing vulgar about her. The men around him had stopped leering, and were staring at her more in wonder than in lust. In another setting, she could have put on the same performance for the Mothers' Union, and would have held them in the palm of her hand.

With the spotlight firmly fixed on her, Isla was determined to put on the best show possible for Chrissie. There had been one brief disturbance. She had been in the middle of a complicated move—one of several she was trying out for the gym's Christmas display—when someone was thrown out of the club. Chrissie had warned her this could happen, but had also reassured her that security was tight for the girls, so Isla had nothing to worry about.

At the gym Isla was always lost in her routine, but tonight her attention kept wandering, mainly because of the man who had come to lean against a pillar to stare at her. All the men were staring at her, but he was watching with particular intent.

She wasn't sure how she felt about him. He was exotic-looking and powerfully built, but unthreatening, possibly because he possessed an unusual air of dignity and presence. Tall and dark, he was beautifully dressed. His crisp white shirt provided a striking contrast to his exquisitely tailored dark suit, and links that might have been black diamonds glittered at his cuffs. As he obviously wasn't going anywhere she continued on with her routine.

She was safely back in her tiny dressing room when the knock came on the door. 'Yes? Come in…'

She was halfway changed, with her jeans and boots on, and grabbed a robe to throw over her bra. She was expecting a visitor. One of the girls had promised to drop off Chrissie's schedule for the next week.

'Oh!'

Shooting out of her seat when she saw the man,

she backed instinctively against the wall with fear lapping over her. It was an old fear, but no less severe for being a haunting memory from the past. One, thankfully failed, sexual assault had left Isla with an instinctive fear of men. That it had happened after her mother's funeral when her emotions were strung out had made the fall-out all the keener. Dragging in a shaking breath, she reminded herself that security was only a shout away.

'Forgive me if I startled you,' the man who had been leaning against the pillar murmured in a deep, intriguingly accented voice. 'They said I'd find you here.'

She calmed herself, telling herself rationally that every man wasn't out to hurt her. She also had to think about Chrissie, who depended on this job. She wasn't going to make a fuss unless she had to.

And, if she had to, she could shout louder than most.

'Can I help you?' she demanded in a tone that sounded scratchy and tense. The man seemed to take up most of the available space in the small room, so there was nowhere else for him to be but close. He was a stunning-looking individual, not that that made it any easier to be alone with him.

'I wanted to apologise for the disturbance to your act.' His dark stare remained steady on her face. 'A man was ejected from the club while you were dancing. You're very good at your work, and I wanted to say how sorry I am for the interruption.'

'Thank you.' Smiling thinly, she reached for the door handle to show him out.

'May I give you a lift home?'

Her eyes widened in shock. 'Oh, no, thank you. I catch the bus. But, thank you for the offer.'

'You catch the bus alone at night?' he demanded, frowning.

His reaction brought a faint smile to her lips. 'Public transport in London is quite safe. The bus drops me at my door.'

'I see.'

He was still frowning, giving her the sense that this was a man who was used to being obeyed.

He might be a devastatingly good-looking individual with an air of command and a custom-made suit, but she was an independent woman who could look after herself.

'So. No lift?' he queried, raising a brow as if he thought he could change her mind.

'No lift,' she confirmed. She had a keen sense of self-preservation. She always had her bus fare home, and she would be using it tonight.

'Perhaps I'll see you again,' he suggested.

'Perhaps,' she agreed lightly. Taking a firmer

hold of the door handle, she swung the door wide and stood aside.

'Goodnight, Isla.'

Alarm bells rang. 'You know my name?'

His firm mouth slanted. 'The manager told me when I asked to speak to you.'

Isla's brain cogs whirred. The manager would not allow a customer near a girl without a very good reason. So what was this man's excuse? Making an apology for a disturbance at the club? She didn't think so.

'Who are you?' she demanded, feeling unsettled, as well as slightly annoyed by this blatant breach of club protocol.

Her question seemed to amuse him. 'My friends call me Shaz.'

'Goodnight, Shaz,' she said pointedly.

She remained outside the door, pressed against the wall, wanting to keep some distance between them. The fact that he had made enquiries about her had only added to her unease—that and his sheer, brutal machismo.

'Goodnight, Isla.'

His eyes had turned warm and humorous, prompting her to soften enough to say, 'I'm glad you enjoyed the show.'

Her body tingled when he gave her one last appraising look. She was relieved he was leaving, and yet almost regretful knowing they would never meet again. When he rested his hands lightly on her upper arm, she gasped out loud, but he wasn't done with her yet. Leaning forward, he brushed his lips against her cheek—first her right cheek and then the left.

Kissing on both cheeks was the usual greeting and leave-taking gesture in many countries across the world, she reminded herself as her heart went crazy, both with alarm, and something else.

Pulling herself together fast, she moved out of his way and stood stiffly to attention as he left. Her senses were in turmoil. Wherever life took her from here on in, the man in the club wouldn't be easy to forget.

CHAPTER TWO

SINISTER HIGH-POWERED LAUNCHES announced the arrival of the Sheikh's team. The lead launch was sleek and black, while smaller vessels swarmed like mosquitoes in attendance as they cut a foaming path up the River Thames. The vessels were all heading for the same pontoon, about a hundred or so yards from the café where Isla was working at one of several part-time jobs that helped to pay her tuition fees at the university.

'Hey, Chrissie—come and look at this,' she called out.

Staff and customers alike were held riveted by the sight of the fleet arriving. A sight like this was just what Chrissie needed to cheer her up. The family emergency had been resolved—sort of—but Chrissie was still worried to death about her father, who had been brought home by the police after being arrested for drunk and disorderly conduct. The only blessing was that last night had ended so well for both girls, with a better than expected pay-out from the club.

A mystery benefactor had left the extra money, the manager had explained to Isla, to make up for the disturbance at the club. She guessed it must have been the man who had introduced himself. The money couldn't have come at a better time, as she had been able to hand it all over to Chrissie to pay her father's fine.

That wasn't the only good thing about last night, Isla recalled, touching her cheek. It was the first time in years she'd come into contact with a man who hadn't given her the creeps, and this was especially odd, as the man last night had been a paean to masculinity.

It was just a kiss.

Yes, but it was a kiss she would never forget.

'What's up?' Chrissie said, joining Isla at the window. 'Oh, wow…'

Isla rubbed her sleeve across the heat-misted window so they could both get a better view of the powerboats as they slowed in preparation for docking. She was glad to see Chrissie looking more relaxed as they crushed up comfortably against each other. Just dealing with the fine had been some consolation, though the problem with Chrissie's father was unlikely to go away.

Men were leaping ashore to secure the ropes on a pontoon as new as the fantastic new development springing up next door to the café. This was all part of the same Thames-side university campus being funded by His Serene Majesty, Sheikh Shazim bin Khalifa al Q'Aqabi, a legendary philanthropic figure in a world weary of shallow celebrity. At thirty-five, the Sheikh was not just one of the richest men in the world, but was also practically invisible to the media. His immense power and wealth allowed him to remain beneath the avid radar of celebrity, which made any sighting of him all the more exciting. The new buildings he was funding included a veterinary science department, which Isla was particularly excited about as she had recently won the most amazing prize for her research project into endangered species. The prize included a trip to the Sheikh's desert kingdom of Q'Aqabi to see for herself his world-beating nature reserve. And to work there one day, she hoped.

'Isla! Chrissie! Stop daydreaming and get back to work!'

Both girls jumped into action as their boss, Charlie, yelled at them. Prize winner or not, Isla was still impoverished after so many years of study. She had yet to secure her first position as a veterinary surgeon and, like many students, her finances were precariously balanced. If she lost even one of her part-time jobs her future career could be in jeopardy.

The activity at the pontoon proved addictive, and Isla glanced repeatedly out of the window as she worked. The uniformed crew had moored up, and rain had begun to pelt down as a party of men disembarked. Dressed disappointingly in traditional western work clothes, rather than the flowing robes of her imagination, they strode up the pontoon in arrow formation towards the building site.

'Do you think the Sheikh's at the head of them?' Chrissie asked, breaking Isla's spell as she leaned against her.

'Who knows?' Isla replied, studying the figure in the lead. He was too far away to see his features clearly, but there was something about him—

'Isla—Chrissie,' Charlie called out sharply, reminding both girls that there was work to be done. 'Get that order for the Sheikh's team together now!'

Flashing a willing smile in Charlie's direction, Isla hurried to obey. The Sheikh's office had called ahead to make sure that an order of coffee was delivered to site as soon as the Sheikh's team arrived.

'I don't think he's with them,' she whispered to Chrissie as she squeezed past her friend behind the counter. 'I expect he has more important things to do.'

'More important than supervising the building of his new facility?' Chrissie's expressive mouth pressed down with amazement as she shrugged. 'Seems to me, he should be here, if only to make sure his billions aren't wasted on coffee.'

Isla laughed. 'They won't be wasted. The new vet school is going to be amazing. I've seen the plans in the university library.' And it was Isla's dream to be part of those plans. Endangered species were her passion, and she was aching to do what she could to help out. The thought that very soon she would be flying thousands of miles to the magical-sounding kingdom of Q'Aqabi to visit the Sheikh's nature reserve still seemed like a fantasy too far—

'Isla!'

'Coming,' she promised Charlie.

'I'll take it,' she added to Chrissie, grabbing the cardboard tray that was waiting to be loaded with coffee.

'Knowing your luck, the Sheikh will be there,' Chrissie complained, pulling a comic face. 'I can just see the drama unfolding now: the fast-food flirt and the autocratic Sheikh. That should be a fun ride, shouldn't it?'

'After last night?' Isla grimaced. 'I'm all for the quiet life. I don't want any more hunter-gatherers pushing me over the threshold from safe to insanity.'

'It wasn't so bad,' Chrissie pointed out. 'You met a great guy—'

'I said, I met a guy—'

'Don't tinker with the detail. Main thing is, we got paid a fortune.'

'Danger money.' Isla laughed, hiding the fact that it had taken more than Chrissie would ever know for her to shed her clothes in front of a room full of men. The fact that Isla's brush with the sickening danger of a sexual assault had happened years ago had left her no less wary. 'And I'm not a flirt. I'm just friendly,' she teased before Chrissie could see the shadow of that memory in her eyes.

'Whatever,' Chrissie intoned with a wry look. 'You get bigger tips than me, that's all I know.'

'Which I share,' Isla reminded her friend with a laugh. 'And, as for the Sheikh—I doubt we'll ever see him. If he comes to cut the ribbon when his new building is opened, I'll be surpri—'

'Will you girls stop gossiping and get back to work?' Charlie rapped impatiently.

Exchanging glances, both girls quickly returned to their duties. Chrissie busied herself with the orders on hand, while Isla reluctantly shoved all thoughts of the exciting projects and sheikhs to one side so she could concentrate on finishing the coffee order for the building site.

'Isn't your shift almost over?' she asked Chrissie as they bustled past each other.

'Yes, Mum,' Chrissie teased with a wink. 'But I'm happy to stay on while there's a rush and you're taking that outside. I can't afford to lose this job.'

'I can't afford to lose any of my jobs,' Isla agreed.

They shared a rueful grin. Juggling studies and holding down multiple jobs wasn't easy for either girl, though, while Chrissie had the looks and figure to strut her stuff for loads of money at the pole-dancing club, Isla's second job was working quietly in the university library. That was when she wasn't working her third job, teaching basic gymnastics to keen youngsters in the gym. Not that she was complaining. She loved the quiet of the library, where she could snatch a study break along with her lunch, while the children in the after-school gym club kept her fit and motivated with their enthusiasm—

'Isla!'

'Yes, boss!' Conscious that Charlie was watching her, she quickly loaded the last of the coffees. 'The site order is ready to go.'

'Then, get it out there before the coffee gets cold,' Charlie grumbled, doing his best to look as if he'd just sucked on a lemon.

Glancing at the rain battering the windows,

Isla grabbed her jacket and tugged it on. 'Yes, boss—'

'This is a coffee shop, not gossip central,' Charlie grouched, deepening his frown as she walked past him.

She countered Charlie's bad mood with one of her usual cheery smiles. 'You know you love me, really.'

'The only reason I employ you is for that smile,' Charlie grudgingly admitted.

'That man,' Chrissie exploded. 'Who does he think we are? Smiling puppets?'

'Employees?' Isla suggested with her usual good humour. 'We need this job, Chrissie,' she discreetly reminded her hot-headed friend.

'You're going to get soaked,' Chrissie objected, brow wrinkling thunderously as she stared out of the window.

'Yes,' Isla agreed, 'but, the sooner I get out there, the sooner I get back.'

'Okay, Ms Capability—say hi to the Sheikh, if you see him.'

'Like I'm going to get close.'

'If he's there he'll have security surrounding him,' Chrissie agreed. 'Oh, well, you can still drop a few hints to his team that you're a star student at the university, and you'll be over in Q'Aqabi very soon, when you'll be only too glad to offer your services—'

'I beg your pardon?' Isla acted shocked.

'Okay, Miss Prim—you know what I'm talking about. Get out there before the coffee goes cold. And don't forget to drop that hint,' Chrissie called after her.

Was she wrong to hope that, if the Sheikh had chosen to visit his billion-dollar building site, the white-chocolate mocha with the extra caramel shot and a double squirt of cream wasn't destined for him? Isla smiled as Charlie opened the door for her. A girl had to have her fantasies, and Isla's involved real tough-guy sheikhs—impossibly handsome, riding imperious white stallions... The Sheikh would be clad in flowing robes, and he would live in a Bedouin tent that billowed gently in the warm desert breeze—

'You're lucky I don't dock you girls' dreaming time from your wages,' Charlie rapped as she went past him. 'If you don't watch out, I'll charge you for breakfast.'

Charlie was a kind old thing really, with a bark that was far worse than his bite. And no way was she going to lose out on breakfast, when it was her one decent meal of the day.

Head down, she speed-walked through the driving rain to the mud bath next door. There was no easy way to walk across a building site other than to do it as fast as she could without spilling the coffee.

'Stop!'

She stopped dead and almost dropped the tray. She had reached a steel mesh gate manned by an unsmiling security guard, but, as the gate was open, she had walked straight through.

'You're not allowed on the site,' the guard informed her brusquely.

'But I have instructions to be here,' she tried to explain.

'No one is allowed on the site without protective clothing. And I have to check your identity—'

As the guard reached towards her she flinched. An instinctive reaction. Just one of the many leftover side effects from the attempted assault… It made her creep to have any man touch her, with the exception of Charlie, who was like a grumpy old uncle, and the man in the club last night—

'I'll take over here.'

She jerked alert as a second man spoke. *Oh, no! Shoot me and bury me now.* 'It's you,' she said lamely, recognising the man from the club.

'Quite a surprise,' he agreed drily, and with maximum understatement. 'I'll see to this,' he said, dismissing the guard.

The guard's reaction was impressive. He practically stood to attention and saluted. 'Yes, sir,' he said, taking a giant step back.

Before she had chance to say anything, two strong arms had snapped around her waist.

'What are you doing?' was about all she could manage as the air shot from her lungs. She had to concentrate on balancing the coffee as the giant of a man led her away. And, for the second time, strangely, there was no fear, no creeps, just quite a lot of affront that the people on the site were making it so hard for her to deliver coffee.

'I'll drop the tray if you don't slow down.'

Not that it would do him any harm in his steel-capped boots. Gone were the black silk socks and highly polished shoes and in their place was a hard hat and a high-vis' jacket. If he'd seemed big last night, he was positively enormous now. And he didn't look the type to yowl if hot coffee should happen to land on his naked skin.

His naked skin...

Stop that now!

She had never known anything like it. Her mind was permanently closed to all thoughts of men's physical attributes—or so she'd thought up to last night. And now she had enough to do, balancing a tray of red-hot coffee while keeping up with the man's ground-eating stride. By the time they reached one of several mobile homes on the site, she was well and truly rattled, and when he angled his chin towards the door she stopped dead and refused to go a step further.

Reaching in front of her, he opened the door.

Jerking his chin, he indicated that she should go first.

'Everyone on the site has to wear proper clothing and carry a security pass,' he explained. 'Health and safety,' he added brusquely.

She stalled, playing for time. She didn't feel uncomfortable with him, as she had with other men, but going into a building where she would be alone with him was a step too far. 'I've never encountered a problem before,' she protested with some justification. 'Like most of the people at the university, I use the building site as a cut-through when I'm walking between the campus and the café.'

'That doesn't make it right,' he said flatly with a stare that ripped through her like a shot of adrenaline. Since he'd arrived, things had obviously been tightened up. She'd spread the word.

The sooner she left the coffee, the sooner she was out of here, but she couldn't deny that the all-embracing warmth inside the mobile building was welcome. The man called Shaz had started rifling through a rail of high-vis' jackets. Blowing on her hands, she wondered if he felt the cold. As part of the Sheikh's team, she guessed he didn't have to suffer it for too much of the year.

'Here—try this one,' he said, holding out a jacket.

Seeing her difficulty, he took the tray of coffee, brushing his hand against her frozen skin as he did so. 'It should be better,' he murmured, holding her gaze a disturbing beat too long. 'This one is smaller.'

He put the tray down and then came back to help her out of her wet coat. This time his hand brushed her neck. She had just moved her wet hair out of the way, leaving her skin exposed. It was an accident, she told herself firmly. It had to be an accident.

Leaving her to fasten the jacket, he started work on her security pass.

'Is there anything else you need?' she asked politely.

He raised his head and stared at her. 'Should there be anything else?'

The expression in his eyes pinned her. He was definitely interested—no doubt about it—and he was curious about her, which made her skin prickle. He had the most incredible eyes, and it wasn't just the fact that they were dark, and heavily fringed with jet-black lashes—they were quite simply the most expressive eyes she'd ever seen...and right now, they were warming as he stared at her.

'A pastry, perhaps?' she suggested with a gulp.

With a faintly amused look, he turned back to his work. 'I'll need a photograph,' he said, coming to stand between her and the door.

He fixed her printed image inside the pass. 'You'll need this next time you visit the site,' he explained, pressing it into her hand. The brief moment of connection between them sent a sizzle up her arm.

Closing her hand around the pass, she stepped back. 'It might not be me bringing out the coffee for you next time,' she felt it only fair to point out.

'It will be you,' he stated. His face grew grim. 'I have no intention of equipping every member of staff at the café with a pass and protective clothing.'

'So I drew the lucky straw,' she commented ruefully.

'Seems so,' he agreed. His expression softened minutely.

'Thank you, anyway.' She slung the lanyard holding the pass around her neck.

'Wear it every time you visit the site,' he said, standing up to tower over her.

'I will.' If she ever visited the site again. By now her curiosity was well and truly piqued. Who was he? He was obviously important enough to be in overall command of the site—an architect, perhaps, though his hands were a little rough for that. He was no stranger to manual work. She liked that idea. She had this irrational belief that a down-to-earth man would be safer and, though he certainly looked tough enough to handle a team of men, he didn't strike her as a man who would ever resort to bullying tactics.

'Thanks for the coffee,' he said as she turned to go.

She flinched back, then realised that he was only stepping forward so he could reach out and turn her badge around, so her details were facing outwards.

He raised a brow at her overreaction. 'Protective clothing,' he reminded her. 'Wear it every time you come to the site.'

Her heart thundered a tattoo at the instruction. She guessed he was the type of man who would be accustomed to provoking a reaction in susceptible females. It was just that she had never thought herself a susceptible female before. She was more the plain, forthright variety...

'Boots might be a problem,' he said, bringing her back down to earth with a bump.

'I'm only walking through the mud, not laying bricks,' she said, frowning as she followed his stare to her feet.

His expression instantly hardened, as if no one argued with him.

'Honestly,' she added, softening her comment with a smile, 'I think you can safely forget about boots. And hats,' she added as his stare switched to the row of yellow hard hats lined up on a shelf.

'I'm sure there must be something in your rule book that allows visitors a certain leeway...?'

He turned to stare at her with real interest in his eyes—interest that sent shock waves rolling through her, but then he curved the suspicion of a smile as if his affront at her rebellion had turned to grudging admiration. 'You do have tiny feet,' he allowed, 'and a lot of very long hair to fit comfortably beneath the hat.' He paused a moment, while she got used to the idea that he had given her a pretty thorough once-over, and was remembering her long hair from the club last night, as it was currently screwed up in a work-appropriate do on top of her head. 'Though the high-vis' jacket will keep you warm if it's raining when you come out here again.'

And he cared.

She shuddered in a breath as he took the sides of the jacket in both hands and settled it properly on her shoulders. It was as if he were touching her naked skin, rather than the heavy waterproof jacket. He was so careful with her, and yet his touch was firm and sure.

'You are tiny,' he said.

She frowned a little at that. No one in their right mind would call her tiny. Though, compared to him...

Her cheeks flushed red as he stood back. His gaze lingered on her face, and for a moment she didn't know what to say or do. She sucked in a swift breath as he reached out to brush some damp straggles of hair from her face. She had not expected that and, for once in her life, found herself wishing she were beautiful. Usually she didn't care one way or the other about her looks, or lack of them, but for once it would have been nice to have a man brush wet hair from her face because he wanted to take a better look at her, rather than simply keeping her hair out of her eyes. If she had been beautiful, maybe she could have progressed a fantasy into a moment of pure romance: the chance meeting, love at first sight, and with a man who wouldn't be rough with her—

'That's it,' he said with finality.

His sharp tone brought her back to reality. Checking the fastening on the jacket, she raised the hood, ready to step out into the rain.

'Excellent,' he approved in a tone that suggested he had also sprung back into work mode.

She had definitely overstayed her welcome. But as she hurried to the door she managed to trip over a table—or would have done if he hadn't reached out whip-fast to catch her. She rested for a moment, startled in his arms, and only realised when he settled her back on her feet that she hadn't felt threatened by him at all.

CHAPTER THREE

A GREY DAY in London had taken on a rosy hue, thanks to the unexpected reappearance of a woman who had intrigued him from the first moment he saw her. From pole-dancer to barista was quite a journey. Whether the rush of blood to Isla's cheeks was awareness of him and how close they were standing, or pique that she had only been doing as his office had requested, delivering coffee, when he had ordered her off site for a breach of Health and Safety regs—

Health and Safety regs?

Was that why his hands had expertly skimmed her body? He already knew what lay beneath the bulky safety jacket. Her fuller figure was his ideal. The temptation to back her against the door and strip her down to last night's curves was overwhelming—fortunately, there wasn't time and he had more sense. The one thing that did amuse him was the thought that if Isla had known who he was, he doubted it would have made a jot of difference. This was not a woman to be wooed with status and wealth. She liked you or she didn't. And right now, she didn't.

'Do you mind?' she said, pushing him away.

That in itself was an intriguing first for him. For such a self-possessed woman—and he had to remind himself that this was the same woman who had conducted herself with such dignity in the undignified surroundings of the club—she was surprisingly jumpy, acting almost like an innocent now that they were one to one.

Yes. He'd stopped her falling; Isla allowed with an appropriate amount of gratitude as she brushed herself down. *But, let's not get carried away.* He couldn't hold onto her until her bones turned to jelly, and she had no more sense in her head than a moth flying into a flame. She flashed a warning stare—and had to acknowledge that he was a gentleman, as he'd let her go. And fate had dealt him a more than generous hand. Douse any other man in a rainstorm, and they would look like a drowned rat. Douse this man and he still looked spectacular. His thick black hair glistened with raindrops, while her hair was plastered to her face—and she probably had panda eyes from knuckling rainwater out of them.

'Here, Isla…take it.'

She stared at the money in his hand.

'It's the least I can do,' he insisted, thrusting a wad of notes towards her.

'There's no need for that. I'm just doing my job.'

The job you want to keep?

'I don't mean to be rude,' she added. 'If you would like to leave some money at the end of the week for everyone at the café to share, that would be great.'

What was she doing? Could she afford to turn down such a generous tip?

No. Absolutely not, but something felt wrong about accepting such a large tip from a man she hardly knew—and particularly from this man. It was too much, and after last night at the club when she suspected he had doubled Chrissie's pay, she couldn't take any more from him.

Cut him some slack, Isla's inner voice intoned wearily. *No doubt everyone who works for the fabulously wealthy Sheikh has more money than they know what to do with.*

Maybe. But that wasn't the point. A small show of gratitude was acceptable, but flashing a twenty? She wasn't comfortable with that.

'Thanks anyway…' She shot him a thin smile and left it at that before braving the icy wind with the memory of his fleeting touches branded onto her mind.

Knocking mud off her boots, she walked with

relief into the steamy heat of the busy café. It was good to be back on familiar ground. She felt safe from conflicting feelings here. The customers liked her and she liked them. Charlie said she invited confidences with her easy manner. The truth was Isla needed company as much as anyone else. Since losing her mother and paying off all their debts, she had lived alone in one room above a shop, and she loved the contrast of her busy life at the café. All that company and chat, with breakfast thrown in? What was not to love?

Customers that shook her up, like the man from the building site?

She should forget him. He'd probably be gone by tomorrow.

Forget him?

Maybe not, but she would do her best to keep her mind on the job.

The aromatic air inside the café made Isla's mouth water. Charlie was a good cook and he fed his staff well. No wonder she was smiling, when she had such a great day to look forward to. Once she finished her shift here, she was due at the university gym. Gymnastics had been one of Isla's childhood passions in the days before her father walked out and her mother got sick, and now she was grateful to make money out of her skill. She worked every hour she could to fulfil her mother's dying wish and make her proud.

'My shift is nearly over,' Chrissie carolled happily as she joined Isla at the counter.

'Mine too,' Isla said with a grin.

After the gymnastics classes she could look forward to a long, peaceful evening. That might involve wearing every jumper she possessed with her feet drawn up as close as she dared to her three-bar electric fire, but at least she had a home to go to. A quick glance at Charlie to let him know that she was back was repaid by a hard stare. Understandably. She'd been gone a long time. But once Charlie took in her new outfit, he began to smile. Charlie wasn't the only one. She was so wet, and it was so hot in the café that her clothes were starting to steam. Tipping Charlie a wry look, she explained what had kept her so long. 'I'm to be the Sheikh's team's regular gofer. I think they're going to need lots of coffee while they're here.'

Charlie was pleased to hear it. 'Well done for encouraging business.'

'And look out for the Sheikh when you go back next time,' Chrissie called out.

'Of course I will,' Isla teased Chrissie. Privately, Isla doubted that the Sheikh would be seen until His Royal Sereneness turned up to cut the ribbon on his new buildings and declare them open. In her imagination, the Sheikh of Q'Aqabi was as hard as nails, as rich as Croesus, and as tall, dark and sinister as could be—but compulsively enthralling, all the same.

Realistically, Isla reflected as she got back to her work, the Sheikh was probably shrivelled, pot-bellied, and grumpier than Charlie.

Young. Challenging. Proud. Interesting. But too innocent for him, and he didn't have time to waste on challenges. Interesting? Isla was certainly interesting.

Would he pursue his interest in her further?

Stuffing the twenty away in the back pocket of his jeans, he stared after her. She was proud, and he got that. She'd been offended by money. How would she react if he offered more? Money could buy most things in his world...

But could it buy him everything he wanted?

He doubted that any amount of money could buy Isla. Her grey eyes had flashed fire when she'd seen the twenty. She'd no doubt guessed he was responsible for padding her wages last night. She was resourceful and adaptable. She was also an innocent who had trespassed unwittingly into his dark, sensual world. He wondered about her past experience with men. She was attractive, so there must have been some, though her air of innocence suggested that none had breached either the defences of her body or her heart. He should know better than to play games with a girl like that, but she attracted him. Mild on the outside, she reminded him of a volcano about to erupt, and he wanted to be there when that happened.

He found her beautiful, with that particular peach-like complexion so common in this part of the world. Her hair was rain-soaked, but he remembered it from the club, when it had been long and unruly, and had glittered gold beneath the lights. Her eyes were grey and expressive. Small and lush, she warmed him in a way he hadn't been warmed in a long time, and her strength of character warned there would never be a dull moment. He liked that idea. As a mistress, she showed definite potential, but could he take her innocence and then discard her when he'd had enough?

A casual affair was unthinkable for him. He had everything to prove to his country. His reckless youth, and the tragedy that had detonated, would take a lifetime to repay. He would do nothing to rattle the sound foundations he was building in Q'Aqabi. His duty was to find a suitable bride. He did not have time to waste thinking about a new mistress. He must harden his heart to Isla, even as another part of him hardened in lust.

He summoned his colleagues in the hope that work would distract him, but, however many lectures he gave himself on the subject of forgetting

Isla, he couldn't help but anticipate the next coffee break, and another encounter with the spirited barista.

She didn't go back to the building site. She came up with another plan. Coffee could be left with the security guard, and he could deliver it. Charlie readily agreed to this. They were so busy, he couldn't spare his staff for any more lengthy visits.

The following day Chrissie took over for her, as Isla had to be at the library. She wasn't exactly avoiding a certain person, but she wasn't exactly courting trouble, either. She wasn't used to handling such a compelling man, and she didn't want to appear as if she was overly interested in him. She had the best of excuses. As the prize winner, she was expected to be on duty at the library when the Sheikh of Q'Aqabi finally arrived to tour the university facilities. The head librarian welcomed her with particular enthusiasm as Isla knew more than most about successful breeding programmes of endangered species, having majored in that subject on her course.

The Sheikh's visit had provoked great excitement, and Isla was up earlier than usual getting ready for her duties at the library. She didn't want to let anyone down.

Having tied her hair back neatly, she viewed

her pale face in the mirror. She'd missed sparring with the tough guy from the building site, but today wasn't a day for daydreams, but a day when she could do something to help repay the university that had been so good to her. Checking the lapels on her plain grey suit, she told herself firmly that her racing pulse had everything to do with finally meeting 'the invisible Sheikh', and nothing at all to do with the fact that she might have to cross the building site to get a coffee at some point in the day.

To give herself confidence, she slipped on her red high-heeled shoes. She loved them. They were a sale buy, and so unlike her, but what better day to wear them than today?

She wasn't the only one who was excited, Isla discovered when she arrived at the library and the air of anticipation was infectious. It had transformed the customary silence of the hallowed halls into a tense and expectant waiting room.

The Sheikh of Q'Aqabi was pouring money into the university, and had donated several ancient manuscripts from his private collection. The head librarian explained that he would want to view them, and that was where Isla would step in.

She glanced at the entrance doors yet again. Whatever he looked like, the Sheikh was obviously a fascinating man. Closing her eyes, she drew a steadying breath. Being in the library usually soothed her, but not today. And then she heard a buzz of conversation, heralding the arrival of the vice chancellor and his party. She prepared herself for the sight of a sheikh dressed in flowing robes, and was quite disappointed when the tweedy academics arrived with a group of men in business suits.

But spearheading that group was—

She lurched to her feet, the scrape of her chair screeching through the silence.

Everyone turned to look at her. The man from the building site stared straight at her as if she were the only thing of interest in the entire, echoing space.

Why hadn't he said?

Why was she so slow on the uptake?

She realised now that the man who had told her to call him Shaz was, in fact, His Serene Majesty, Sheikh Shazim bin Khalifa al Q'Aqabi, the major benefactor of the university, and her number one sparring partner.

And he was definitely not pot-bellied, or shrivelled, nor could his expression be called grumpy. Commanding, maybe. Faintly amused, definitely. And no wonder when he'd seen her in so many guises.

Maybe he'd known all along. Maybe he'd been playing games with her. His security team had surely supplied His Majesty with a full break-down of everyone he was likely to meet on cam-pus.

And now he was here in *her* library—the place she loved and felt safest and most at home in; the world of books, where adventures were safely contained within their pages—

There was nothing safe in His Majesty's eyes.

She stood stiffly as he approached, glad that he couldn't hear her heart beating.

'Your Majesty…' She couldn't quite bring her-self to curtsey.

'No need to curtsey.'

Her head shot up, and they exchanged a look—challenge, repaid by challenge. She could see the burn of humour in his dark, luminous eyes. He'd known she wouldn't curtsey—and not because her manners were lacking in any way, but because she was frozen to the spot with surprise, and every inch of her was tingling with awareness.

'And here we have our very own Athena,' the vice chancellor stated with enthusiasm, forcing Isla to break eye contact with the royal visitor.

She was standing to attention like a soldier on parade, she realised, trying to relax. She was never this tense. Forcing herself to look into *His Majesty's* mocking eyes, she saw the flare of cal-culation in them as the vice chancellor continued to sing her praises.

'Isla is our goddess of good order and wisdom, as well as strength and strategy,' the vice chancellor continued, warming to his theme.

'And warfare,' the Sheikh added in an all too familiar husky tone with the faintest tug of a smile at one corner of his mouth. 'Athena was also the goddess of warfare,' he explained with a lift of his brow when Isla shot him a look.

'You two know each other?' The vice chancellor glanced with interest between the two of them.

'We met on the building site,' Isla explained, holding the Sheikh's burning stare steadily. 'I work at the café, Vice Chancellor, and I took out some coffee for His Majesty's team, though I had no idea who he was at the time.' Her stare sharpened on *His Majesty's* amused eyes.

'And would your manner have changed, if you had known?' the ruler of Q'Aqabi enquired mildly.

She thought it better not to answer that.

'Forgive me, Your Majesty,' the vice chancellor interrupted, obviously keen to break the awkward silence. 'Please allow me to formally present Isla Sinclair…'

For a second time, Isla dipped her head politely without sweeping the impressive giant standing in front of her a submissive curtsey.

'You two may well be working together,' the

vice chancellor said with delight, oblivious to Isla's sudden intake of breath. 'Isla is our prize winner, Your Majesty, and, according to the conditions of your very generous gift, Isla will be travelling to Q'Aqabi as part of her prize.'

'Oh, really,' Shaz murmured as if this were news to him. 'My people organised the contest, Vice Chancellor, but be assured that we will welcome you with open arms, Ms Sinclair.'

Isla stared at the hand that Shaz was holding out in formal greeting. She remembered the touch of that hand, and she wasn't too keen on risking the thrill of it with an audience watching.

Muscle up! She was a serious-minded woman; a scientist, a veterinary surgeon—her hand had been all sorts of places. She certainly didn't balk at shaking Shaz's hand, even if she knew now that it had a title attached to it.

'Your Majesty,' she said crisply, giving him a firm handshake.

'Shazim,' he prompted, still holding onto her hand. 'If we're going to be working together we should at least be on first-name terms, Isla.'

'Shazim,' she repeated politely as shock waves travelled up and down her arm. She loved the sound of his name on her lips—and knew she had to pull herself together. But not just yet...

They were still hand-locked when the vice

chancellor coughed discreetly to distract them. Quickly removing her hand from Shazim's grasp, she linked her hands safely behind her back.

'Ms Sinclair thrives on challenge,' the vice chancellor offered with enthusiasm, which didn't exactly help the situation.

'You have some interesting students, Vice Chancellor,' His Majesty commented. 'I'm impressed by how hard some of them, like Isla, work to pay their fees. We must talk more about grants and endowments, so that everyone who wants to can enjoy the benefit of an education here.'

'Whatever you think,' the vice chancellor agreed, flashing a grateful glance at Isla. 'I know Ms Sinclair works harder than most. Apart from her day jobs, Isla holds a gym class in the evenings for the children of parents who work or study here.'

'A gym class?' Shazim's eyes were alive with laughter as he stared down at her, though his face remained commendably still. 'You must need to be supple and fit for that, I imagine, Ms Sinclair?'

'First names, please,' she implored sweetly with a warning flash in her glance. She didn't want to spend the next half an hour trying to reassure the vice chancellor about her pole-dancing exploits at the club.

'Isla runs from praise like a gazelle from a lion,' the vice chancellor praised her with a smile.

'A fitting comparison, Vice Chancellor,' Shazim agreed, flashing her one final mocking look before moving on.

CHAPTER FOUR

IT HADN'T ESCAPED Isla's attention that His Serene Majesty was also known as the Lion of the Desert, but she was no gazelle. She was more of a doughty old warhorse, tough and thick-skinned—

A warhorse?

She was more like a mole blundering blindly about on the fringes of a royal world she knew nothing about, Isla reflected with a frown as she sank down with relief at her desk as the vice chancellor and the royal party moved on. Winning the prize of a trip to Q'Aqabi was the opportunity of a lifetime. She still couldn't quite believe that she'd been chosen. She'd worked so hard, but had always known that it wasn't a guarantee. The opportunity meant everything to her, and she couldn't afford to be distracted by her attraction to Shazim. She had to concentrate on preparing to be plunged into the desert, a world that would test her like no other. She knew it bore no relation to her fantasies, and she welcomed the hardship and danger. She had never been under any illusion where her work was concerned. Working with animals wrenched her emotions this way and that, and Shazim's project would demand every bit of skill she possessed. But if she could do anything to help, she would gladly devote her life to it.

It was hardly likely that they would work together, Isla reassured herself. The Sheikh of Q'Aqabi must have royal duties by the score—

She sprang to her feet as the official party came into view again.

'Coffee time,' the vice chancellor carolled with enthusiasm, rubbing his hands together in anticipation.

'You will excuse me, Vice Chancellor, I hope?' His Majesty intoned graciously. 'I have a wish to see my manuscripts.'

Isla's heart beat like crazy as Shazim stared at her. He must know that she had been detailed to show him the exhibits.

The tiniest adjustment to Shazim's glance was enough to turn his congenial exchange with the vice chancellor into something very different for her. He could seduce her with a look—if she were a different woman. Though she was surprised that the Lion of the Desert was interested in her at all.

'Of course Isla must accompany you,' the vice

chancellor enthused. 'You couldn't have anyone better to accompany you, Your Majesty. I have it on good authority from the head librarian here that Isla brings order to our questing minds.'

'Indeed?' Shazim queried, staring at her with veiled amusement.

'By which our vice chancellor means that I keep the catalogue here in good order,' Isla explained primly.

Shazim's eyes sparkled with humour as he dipped his head with approval. 'I look forward to learning more about how you maintain such an ordered catalogue.'

As Isla led the way he noticed with interest the sassy heels. Everything about Isla Sinclair intrigued him. More than ever he got the sense of the ice maiden with a molten core. It was that heat that made him want to take her to the furthest reaches of the library, to the shadowy, dusty nooks, where no one ever strayed—

'Your Majesty?' she prompted him. 'The tour?'

'Of course. Please, lead on...' He had become distracted watching her walk away. The high heels made her hips sway rhythmically, while her buttocks strained the seam of her skirt. Discovering that Isla was the prize winner was the worst outcome possible. A short affair could be managed discreetly, but she was coming to Q'Aqabi, not just to tour the nature reserve and veterinary facilities as part of her prize, but to offer her expertise and work there for a while. Under those circumstances, there could be no affair, short or otherwise.

'And here we have the illuminated manuscript of the Canticle of...'

He wasn't listening. He knew everything there was to know about the manuscript. Isla could have been spinning him any old yarn, and he'd still be enthralled. His good intentions where restraint was concerned were under pressure already. They were alone in this part of the library, the academic party having moved onto the room where refreshments had been set out. Isla was doing everything she was supposed to, with apparently no personal interest in him. She appeared so contained, when he knew that nothing could be further from the truth. She wasn't docile or tame. Isla was like one of his wild animals, free and spirited. She was ambitious too, and just as driven to succeed as he was. His ambition to be everything he could be to his people to make up for past sins had an obvious cause, but what was driving Isla?

His gaze strayed to her shoes. There was more than a hint of the rebel about her, and he wondered how that would translate in bed.

'I've got a better idea,' he said when she paused in front of a glass cabinet housing another of his priceless illuminated manuscripts.

'Oh?' said, turning with a frown.

'Have dinner with me tonight.'

'What?' She looked at him as if dinner were another word for sex. 'Oh, no, I don't think—'

His suggestion had thrown her. For the first time she was flustered. Her cheeks were red and her breathing sped up. He guessed she wanted to have dinner with him, wanted to spend time with him, but didn't want to do anything to threaten the practical opportunities he could offer Isla in terms of her career.

'I would like to discuss the new veterinary school with you,' he said, making it hard for her to refuse.

'With me?' She touched her chest with surprise, then turned instantly suspicious.

'I would appreciate hearing a recent student's forthright point of view. You would be forthright with me, wouldn't you, Isla?'

'Of course, but—' Her intelligent grey gaze sharpened on his.

'Then, shall we say eight o'clock? I'll have my driver pick you up—'

'But you don't know—'

'Where you live?' Angling his chin, he smiled into her eyes.

'You had me followed?'

He cancelled out her affront with a glance. 'The vice chancellor supplied your address, along

with all other information I might need, so my
people could get in touch with the prize winner
to arrange transport to Q'Aqabi.'

'Of course,' she agreed, biting down on the
swell of her lip as she thought about this.

While Isla settled her mind, he wrestled with
ideas that had never concerned him before. Dis-
creet arrangements could be made when he
wanted a woman in his bed, with mutual agreement the only condition. But when Isla was in
Q'Aqabi where he had duties and responsibilities,
he could not please himself. He was pledged to
his country, and, if he had judged Isla right, she
would want more than a brief affair, and that was
something he could never give her. Would things
change when they reached the desert? Would he
make an exception this one time and mix business with pleasure? Would Isla be prepared to
pay the price for that pleasure, or would it break
her when he sent her away?

And maybe him?

No woman had the power to do that.

His senses sharpened as Isla drew a tense
breath and shook her head. 'I'm afraid dinner
tonight isn't possible.'

'You have a prior engagement?'

'Yes,' she admitted, meeting his gaze with can-
dour, 'with my studies.'

'But that's what I want to talk to you about. I

know your career hopes are pinned on specialising in the preservation of endangered species—'

'Not hopes. I *will* specialise,' she corrected him with a verve he could only admire.

'There is nowhere better than Q'Aqabi for you to pursue your work. We have species on the verge of extinction, and a programme specifically designed to save these animals.'

'Are you offering me a job before I even arrive in the country?'

Her look was both a challenge and a provocation.

'I think I'd better try you out first, to see how you shape up.'

She met his amused stare with distinct lack of humour and a lift of her brow, as if to ask if they were still talking about her career prospects.

The project meant the world to him, and he turned serious as he decided that if Isla was as good as they said she was, she would get the job.

'The team that will be working on my new nature reserve has not been finalised yet, but your up-to-date knowledge and your obvious devotion to your work puts you in a very good position.'

She visibly relaxed, making him wonder again about her past experience with men. When it came to her love of animals, Isla couldn't be shaken, but when it came to flirting with him, it was always one step forward and two steps back.

'You want to have dinner with me,' she confirmed with a frown. 'And this is so we can discuss your nature reserve and the new veterinary school?'

'Amongst other topics,' he agreed. 'I'm sure we won't be short of things to talk about.'

'I hope I don't let you down…'

Even he couldn't be sure, as Isla grew thoughtful, if she was talking about her appeal to him as a person, or as a vet. One thing was certain, he had waited long enough for her answer. 'Do you accept my dinner invitation, or not?'

Her eyes briefly flared, but she had more sense than to take him on. She would not risk antagonising him, when visiting Q'Aqabi was everything she longed for, and had worked so hard to achieve.

'What's your answer, Isla?'

Lifting her chin, she met his stare candidly. 'Thank you, Your Majesty. Yes. I will have dinner with you.'

CHAPTER FIVE

HE WAS JUST relaxing into victory, believing Isla had not only agreed to have dinner with him, but quite a lot more, when she added three crushing words: 'But not tonight.'

'When, then?' he demanded curtly.

'In Q'Aqabi,' she said, delivering her final surprise. 'I'll have dinner with you in Q'Aqabi, when we have worthwhile things to share. I'd only bore you to death otherwise.'

Nothing could be further from the truth.

'Your audacity in refusing the invitation of the man who has donated this prize you care so much about is—'

'Breathtaking?' she agreed, nodding her head. 'Yes, I suppose it must seem that way, but, you see, this course means everything to me.'

'So blackmailing me is your way of showing this?'

'I'm just asking for a chance,' she argued passionately. 'I'm asking for a role in your project—

a real role. I'm begging, actually. I can't afford to be proud when this is all I've ever wanted. And I know I can help you. I've learned all the latest techniques, and I'm certain I can add value to your plans. I'm already excited—'

'Aren't you taking rather a lot for granted?' he interrupted.

'Am I?'

Despair showed in her eyes. He had no intention of withdrawing the prize. According to the vice chancellor, Isla had been an outstanding student, and he didn't doubt she had a lot to offer. Her only downfall was that beneath that cool exterior, she was headstrong and passionate—

Wasn't that what he liked about her?

Everything in his life was predictable and rigidly controlled—by him. Isla had turned everything on its head. And she had other admirable qualities. His most recent information said she had been forced to suspend her studies in order to nurse her sick mother, and when her mother died Isla had moved heaven and earth to find the money to get back on the course. She was undoubtedly a force to be reckoned with, and in time might prove a real asset to his project. She would certainly be an asset in his bed.

He had never concluded a bargain quite like this before. Women wanted his money, his power and his influence. They wanted to share his bed.

They wanted good sex and a trophy lover. Isla wanted his permission to work the hardest shift on earth in the desert alongside his veterinary rangers. For once in his life, he couldn't be sure if she wanted that more than anything else, but he looked forward to finding out.

'Perhaps you should listen to my terms before you get too excited,' he suggested.

'Your terms?' She was instantly wary.

'You will be going to the desert, which is not the place you imagine.' When her face fell, he added, 'It is far, far more beautiful. But it can also be a hellhole,' he warned, his face growing grim as hers grew rapt. 'Paradise one moment, it can be transformed in a matter of minutes into the most dangerous place on earth, and you, as an expert in your field, must learn the ways of the desert, and how to survive it.'

'I'm up to it,' she stated firmly.

'You will be shown everything you need to know. If you don't prove your worth, you will leave.'

'Will you be there?'

He guessed she had spoken without thinking, as her cheeks were now burning red. But would he be in the desert? Would he retrace that reckless youth's footsteps to the site of the tragedy?

'Prove to me that you are the most willing and able of all my recruits, and you can stay on in Q'Aqabi and work with my other willing re-cruits,' he said, moving past the question.

As she gulped convulsively, he guessed that Isla's hidden fiery depths encouraged her to pic-ture harems stuffed to the brim with his *willing recruits*. 'You are the most promising of all the students here,' he said, to put a balm on her vivid imagination, 'or you wouldn't be getting this chance. If your theoretical studies are matched by your practical application of them—'

'Oh!' she said before he even had chance to finish. 'Thank you—thank you!'

It was as if all her tension had released at once, and as she took a step forward she looked for an in-stant as if she was going to fling her arms around him and hug him tight. Fortunately for them both, she curbed the impulse, and remained instead vi-brating with excitement in front of him. Physical contact that wasn't initiated by him was alien in the world he inhabited. He had never known af-fection as a child, having been brought up in a nursery of royal offspring from several wives. His brother had tried to make up for the lack of parental love by being more like a father to him, but his brother had been dead for many years.

He found himself relaxing, even smiling at Isla. Her unselfconscious show of gratitude had touched him more than he'd realised. It had also aroused him.

'Please forgive me, Your Majesty—'

They both turned as the vice chancellor spoke. Shazim couldn't be sure how long the party of academics had been back, but he guessed long enough to see Isla move as if to hug him, as his elderly host was staring at him with concern, no doubt wondering if she had breached royal protocol, and possibly damaged the excellent relationship between Q'Aqabi and the university.

'I hesitate to remind you about our busy schedule,' the vice chancellor ventured, anxiety ringing in his voice.

He quickly reassured the older man. 'You're quite right, Vice Chancellor, and I apologise for taking up so much of Ms Sinclair's valuable time, but she has been a font of information, and a fascinating companion with a novel take on so many things.'

'On that we are agreed,' the vice chancellor told him warmly, his relief clearly visible.

Isla carefully avoided looking at him when the vice chancellor said this.

'She has the highest marks ever recorded,' the vice chancellor added in a conspiratorial stage whisper. 'You couldn't have anyone better on the team.'

'I'm sure you're right,' he said mildly, raising his brow a fraction as he turned to look at Isla—who clearly wasn't sure whether she should smile or remain expressionless beneath the barrage of praise, but at least she didn't simper.

'I won't let you or the university down,' she told them both with feeling.

'I know you won't, my dear. Your Majesty...' Standing back to allow him to go first, the vice chancellor indicated that it was time for them to join the rest of the official party.

'I'll see you in Q'Aqabi, Ms Sinclair,' he murmured.

His senses stirred as Isla lowered her gaze. When she bit her lip, he wondered if she was reflecting on what exactly she had just talked herself into.

She was in trouble and sinking fast, Isla reflected later, swirling a sweetener into the coffee on her desk. Not that she had changed her mind about going to Q'Aqabi. She'd worked her socks off to even get a sniff at the prize. Shazim's offer of a possible job after her visit to his country was like all her best dreams coming true at once. And she would prove herself, whatever it took. Her only question was, could she work with him? Could she see Shazim every day, and not be distracted by thoughts that had no connection with the project that meant so much to both of them?

Look at it this way—you're a newly qualified vet with grime beneath your fingernails, while

Shazim is an all-powerful sheikh with more sex appeal than there are grains of sand in his desert.

They weren't just incompatible, they were quite literally worlds apart. Shazim hadn't answered her question about whether he would be in the desert at the same time she was, but she doubted it somehow. He'd have many other things to do. Of course she wished he would be the one to show her the hidden secrets of the desert. She couldn't ask for anything more than to see the dangerous wilderness through his eyes. But that sensual world of billowing Bedouin tents, and endless passion beneath the stars on the shores of some tranquil oasis with only the sound of the night hawk to disturb them, was just a fantasy, as he had reminded her, and had no bearing on what she was likely to see.

But if she did see anything like that...and if she did spend some time alone in the desert with Shazim...

That wasn't going to happen, but if it did, and if by some incredible chance she learned to trust again and they had an affair, heartache in exchange for all of that didn't seem too bad a deal— at least, not from this safe distance.

Isla's arrival at Q'Aqabi International Airport on a commercial jet was a disappointment. Not because the airport was short of anything, but because it had too much of everything. It was the slickest, most efficient, most opulent and impressive airport terminal Isla had ever been through, when she had hoped for a little romance, and perhaps some mystery and magic.

And there was no sign of Shazim.

Of course there was no sign of Shazim. His Majesty had left London long before her, on his private jet the size of a super-airliner, according to the brief news feature she'd watched, detailing the Sheikh of Q'Aqabi's benevolence towards the university. Did she expect the ruler of the country to roll out the red carpet for one newly qualified vet and her mound of unattractive-looking baggage?

No, but maybe she had expected to detect the hint of sandalwood on the air, and perhaps a few grains of sand on the pristine white marble floor—

And camels instead of cabs?

Get real. This was twenty-first-century oil money, polished to the highest sheen. There was a lake of black gold beneath her feet, and a nature reserve somewhere deep in the desert, waiting for her to start work.

'Welcome to Q'Aqabi, Ms Sinclair—'

She whirled around to see a young woman

around her own age with the friendliest dark, almond-shaped eyes.

'His Majesty has asked me to meet you and show you to the palace...'

The palace?

'My name is Miriam, but my friends call me Millie,' the girl explained.

'Pleased to meet you, Millie.' The two girls smiled as they shook hands. 'I thought I would be staying in a hotel?'

'His Majesty thought that you, as the prize winner, should have the honour of staying at the royal palace.'

Near Shazim? Her heart sank at the reality of being close to him. Dreams were one thing, but this was all too real.

'That's very kind of His Majesty,' she made herself say.

'He is very kind. Our King is the best of men,' Millie assured her, stirring Isla's curiosity as to how Shazim's countrymen saw him. 'And you'll soon be in the desert,' Miriam added, sensing something of Isla's disappointment that she wouldn't be going straight to the reserve. 'Though I expect you're looking forward to the award ceremony tonight.'

'Oh, I am,' Isla enthused, deeply conscious of the honour. 'Will His Majesty be accompanying our party to the desert?' She hoped not, as the only thing in her head was Shazim, clad in flowing robes with the setting sun burning fiery red behind him, when she needed all her concentration on her work.

'I'm not sure,' Millie said—guardedly, Isla thought. 'His Majesty only travels into the desert when it is absolutely necessary.'

'Oh, I see.'

She didn't see at all. The ruler of a desert kingdom who only went into the desert when it was *necessary*? How did Shazim oversee his nature reserve? How did he visit his people in outlying villages? There was some mystery here, and it was one she felt she must get to the bottom of, though for now she had to content herself with climbing into the sleek black limousine so she didn't keep Millie waiting.

Millie said goodbye and closed the door, leaving Isla sealed inside the luxurious interior. She had gained nothing more than a passing impression of snow-white skyscrapers silhouetted against the bluest of skies, before getting into the vehicle. Looking out of the window, she was fascinated by the lush green spaces and wide squares she could see; the view left her with a sense of order and purpose that she told herself could only have been created by Shazim. Everything he did was in honour of his late brother, she had read somewhere, and this immaculate city was certainly a wonderful tribute. It did make her wonder if Shazim was so shackled to duty he made no time for himself. For all his wealth and power, and even his occasional flashes of humour, he had struck her as a remote man.

Her deepening feelings for him worried her. They couldn't go anywhere. She was wasting her time. Worse, she was allowing herself to become distracted, when this trip was so vital to her future. She had to try and put Shazim out of her mind...though how she was going to do that, she had no idea.

Her next concern wasn't as pressing, but it was very real. As the limousine slowed before sweeping through a pair of enormous golden gates, she wished she had worn something more elegant than her practical travelling clothes.

They had arrived at the palace. And, realistically, she didn't think that any outfit would quite match up to it. Craning her neck, she stared out of the window.

The palace was incredibly beautiful, like something out of a fairy tale, with turrets and domes and minarets. The stone—marble, she guessed—was sparkling white and veined in the palest pink. And the building was so vast that, even when she tried looking every which way out of the limousine, she couldn't see all of it.

The driver had stopped the vehicle in front of a

wide sweep of marble steps, where a committee of men and women in flowing robes was waiting to greet her. There was no sign of Shazim, but as the driver opened her door and stood back a man dressed in a long white robe with the traditional headdress, which she had learned before she arrived was called a keffiyeh, stepped forward to greet her.

'His Majesty welcomes you, and hopes you will find your stay here pleasant.'

When he bowed over her hand, rather than shaking it, Isla's throat dried at the enormity of the task that lay ahead of her.

'Please thank His Majesty, and tell him that I am delighted to be here.'

She wasn't used to such formality, and would have to rise to the occasion, Isla realised with mounting apprehension. It was just that everything around her was on such an incredible scale. Nothing could have prepared her for this. She was escorted past guards in jewel-coloured ceremonial robes, with sabres flashing at their sides, and then she was introduced to the personal maid who was to take her onto her suite of rooms.

The splendour inside the palace as they walked deeper into its fragranced interior took her breath away. The exquisite marble, the gilding, the intricate marquetry, the jewels glinting in the doors, and the light, furnishings, space—ceilings stretching away to the heavens, and rooms the size of football pitches, corridors decorated with priceless objets d'art. There were shaded internal courtyards with orange trees and secret nooks where birds carolled as loudly as they would in any park. It was all quite incredible, and far beyond anything her feeble imagination might have conjured up. The talents of countless craftsmen must have been employed to create such a beautiful palace. And, yes, she acknowledged with a secret smile, the scent of sandalwood and spice was everywhere, just as she had always dreamed and hoped it would be.

Once she was installed in her lavish suite of rooms, Isla's major concern turned to what she was wearing for the ceremony. She didn't have any money to spare for new clothes, and had cobbled together an outfit with Chrissie's help. The outfit consisted of the plain grey suit she wore when she was working in the library, with the addition of a cheap lace blouse. She had chosen a pair of sensible low-heeled shoes, and tied her hair back neatly in a low ponytail. The modest outfit had seemed appropriate in England, but here it just looked cheap.

She felt even more uncomfortable when she finally left the relative sanctuary of her suite, accompanied by the group that had been sent to fetch her. They were all decked out in the smartest of uniforms, or robes and silken gowns. She felt like a dowdy sparrow in an aviary packed with birds of paradise.

She told herself firmly that it was time to pull herself together. She wasn't a little girl now, standing outside the kitchen door at Lord and Lady Anconner's house, where her mother had used to work. She was here because she had worked hard to be here, and her life wasn't one of luxury and privilege. She'd be heading out to the desert soon, and that was where the real work would begin.

Her little group stopped at the grand double doors of the hall in which the ceremony was to be held. The doors were entirely made of gold. They stole her breath away, but her big adventure had only just begun. The walls inside the ceremonial chamber were gold, and the floor was marble inlaid with gold. There was a throne at the far end of the room, and that was also gold. A plush red carpet led up the steps to the front of the throne. A shiver of awareness coursed through her, for there, already seated waiting for her in imperial splendour, dressed in flowing robes of unrelieved black, was His Serene Majesty, Sheikh Shazim bin Khalifa al Q'Aqabi.

As her attendants dropped back, trumpeters sounded a fanfare, and she set out on the longest walk of her life.

* * *

He rammed his body back against the throne. Seeing Isla again shook him to the core. Frustration was eating him alive. He was used to satisfying his smallest whim at once, not putting it on hold like this. She looked more beautiful than ever. Her sombre suit was so appropriate for the occasion. His project wasn't flippant in any way, but vitally important, and it deserved the serious approach she had taken. In his view, she couldn't have pitched her appearance any better, and he appreciated the concern she'd shown.

She walked steadily towards him, her gaze fixed on his face. He stood as she mounted the steps, and inhaled deeply when she came to a halt in front of him. He could smell her familiar wildflower scent, and the soap she had used in the shower. She was beautiful. She was special. She was Isla.

'Congratulations,' he said formally, holding out the scroll due to the prize winner. 'I look forward to you bringing new ideas to our work.'

'That is all I want,' she said steadily, staring him straight in the eyes.

'That, and dinner, I imagine?' he prompted in a low voice.

'I beg your pardon?' she murmured so that only he could hear.

'Dinner,' he repeated in the same low tone.

'You do remember your promise back in England—to have dinner with me when we have something to discuss? I think your upcoming journey to the desert merits that, don't you? I imagine you have been studying and planning, and I certainly have a lot of *worthwhile* topics to discuss with you.'

Something flashed in her eyes as he reminded Isla of the phrase she had used at the university as an excuse not to have dinner with him right away, but she quickly masked her feelings. She was too shrewd to throw away her opportunity on a point of pride.

'How gracious of Your Majesty to invite me to eat with you, and give me the opportunity to discuss the nature reserve with you,' she said, bowing her head. 'I would be delighted and honoured to have dinner with you.'

She had brightened and looked more confident. Dinner was harmless, especially when she had no doubt heard of the official banquet tonight, when there would be other notable achievers present. She couldn't know that he had something different in mind.

'I will send for you,' he said.

'At what time?'

He drew a breath. Being questioned wasn't usual for him. He gave an order and it was carried out. 'At nine,' he said abruptly.

'But the banquet's at eight—' She stopped, and he saw understanding flare in her eyes. 'Your Majesty?' she queried.

'Nine o'clock,' he repeated as the trumpeters delivered a closing fanfare, signalling that the ceremony was over, and Ms Sinclair must return to her suite of rooms to ready herself for dinner with the Sheikh.

CHAPTER SIX

HE ORDERED A lavish buffet to be laid out on the balcony overlooking the oasis. With the help of his head gardener, he had personally selected the flowers from his temperature-controlled orangery. There were white roses, blue sapphire-like agapanthus, luxury soft, pink sweet avalanche roses, with peachy spray roses and pink veronica—all the colours of the sunset. Standing back, he took pleasure in the finished effect. The long table was laid with snowy-white linen. Candles glowed in silver sconces, while the finest crystal glittered in the moonlight. They would sit on cushions, as was the custom in his country. Traditional musicians, sitting in a group some distance away, would play softly to an accompaniment of desert cicadas, and the occasional hooting call of an eagle owl. As bats flittered overhead, even he, the most unromantic of men, had to admit that what his team had created for him was breathtaking. He had never gone to so much trouble for anyone before.

'The prize winner must have the best,' he told his chamberlain as the old man bowed his way out of Shazim's presence, taking everyone with him, having checked that everything had been completed to His Majesty's satisfaction. 'Every person who comes here to help Q'Aqabi and the nature reserve must be shown every possible courtesy and gratitude.'

'Yes, Your Majesty,' his elderly advisor agreed in his gently modulated voice. 'I'm sure Ms Sinclair will be most grateful.'

He didn't want her to be grateful. He wanted her to be happy.

One of them should be.

But, would she come?

Why shouldn't she have doubts? He wasn't being completely honest about this dinner *à deux*. Yes. This special night was a gift from him, and from his country, but would he have gone to this trouble for anyone else? There was an official banquet to honour the high achievers, but he had not even stayed at that long enough to eat, and had returned here to be with Isla.

And he couldn't even be sure of her, when any other woman would have rushed to have dinner with His Majesty, the Sheikh.

Old habits died hard, he discovered, as, rather than glancing at his functional, top-end wristwatch, he stared up at the stars, the moon, and their relative positions in the sky. He had shunned desert lore for too long, because that subject, at least contained within a book, had been his brother's preserve. Shazim believed his right to use those skills had died with his brother on the night of the tragedy, but now the ability was back, and the sky was once again his timepiece.

It was nine o'clock. So, where the hell was she?

Luxuriating in an unusual abundance of spare time, Isla was bathing in a scented bath. The bath had been run for her by the same smiling maid who had escorted her to her suite of rooms. There was everything she had ever dreamed of for her comfort. Even the big fluffy towels were softer and warmer, while crystal flacons filled with perfumed oils and emollient milks were things of beauty, rather than functional, like the plastic tubs she was used to. The walls of her bathing chamber—she couldn't even begin to think of it as a bathroom—were lined with lapis lazuli in a rich shade of blue that reminded her of the night sky. Even the taps gleamed silver like the stars. The maid had insisted on lighting hundreds of tiny candles to make the whole process a stunning experience. And now, she discovered, that same maid had laid out several silk chiffon gowns for her to choose from.

'For the heat,' the maid explained in broken

English, with a smile so open and warm Isla couldn't find it in her to refuse.

She had never been treated so well. Her only experience of wealth and privilege had been with her mother's employers, but Lord and Lady Anconner had treated them both like machines—people without feelings, and not worthy of their care.

This was the starkest contrast possible, Isla concluded as she stared with bewilderment at the selection of gowns.

'I'm hopeless at this. I don't have a clue which one to wear—can you help?' she asked the maid, miming her request at the same time. She only owned one dress, and that was the plain grey one she had worn for her graduation. These gowns were in rainbow shades, and she didn't know where to start.

The maid rushed to help, and picked out two. One was in a soft blush rose, the colour of the sky at the horizon at dawn, and the other was a soft blue, decorated with silver.

Either one, the maid mimed back, holding up first one exquisite dress and then the other.

'Which one would you choose?'

The maid held up the sky-blue dress, and, drawing an arc above her head to represent the sky, she next drew the bowl of the sun, from which all life came. Then, she touched her heart, and brushed her stomach with her hand as if she were carrying a child.

Isla tried hard not to let her surprise show. She had to arrive at a decision fast.

'I love the one you've chosen.' But not for the reason the maid had used to make her choice.

Apprehension stormed through her. She was being naive if she thought Shazim had invited her to a private dinner in order to quiz her about her work. It might not seem possible to her that he looked at her with interest in anything other than her professional skills, but to everyone else...

The maid coughed discreetly, and glanced pointedly at the beautiful little French ormolu clock on the console table.

What could she do? She had left it too late to let him down.

He was staring out over the oasis. Flat and empty, it could have been a symbol of his life. It was how he'd seen his life when he lost his brother. Behind him was the table loaded with delicious things, but he couldn't be sure Isla would join him.

His senses flared as he heard her behind him.

'Isla—'

His face as he turned must have betrayed the fact that he wasn't simply greeting the prize winner who could give so much to his country, and to his brother's project, but a woman he wanted in his bed. She looked exquisite and, for a moment, he was too stunned to speak. He had half expected Isla to wear her usual jeans, or perhaps the sober grey suit she had worn for the ceremony, but this most practical of women was floating towards him in the most glamorous gown he had ever seen. Ankle length, it was composed of several layers of the finest silk chiffon that undulated and drifted around her as she moved. And she'd left her hair loose. Did she have any idea how beautiful she was?

He thought not. Isla was as unaffected as the day was long, and as direct and as uncompromising as ever.

The scene he had created for her enjoyment stopped her in her tracks.

'Shazim, this is…'

She started to speak, but for once words failed her and she gestured helplessly instead. 'I can't describe it,' she admitted. 'I had no idea there was an oasis behind the palace, and this candlelit setting against the night sky is just so unbelievably beautiful. I had no idea you could be so romantic,' she added as she took it all in.

'My team are responsible,' he retorted with a self-deprecating shrug. 'They wanted our prize winner to have the best experience possible while she's here.'

He couldn't even speak of her as if this was his idea, and Isla was standing in front of him. His heart was ice. He had flashes of longing to be different, but the ice must stay. He didn't deserve anything more.

'You've gone to far too much trouble—or your team has,' Isla insisted. 'But I'm really grateful.'

From the little he had come to know of her, he knew how pragmatic a woman she was, and so he was surprised to hear the shake in her voice, as if she had been touched by the effort that had been gone to on her behalf, so maybe Isla had problems demonstrating her feelings too.

Or maybe the trouble he had gone to made her nervous. There was that possibility too.

'Please thank your team for me,' she said, polite as ever as she leaned forward to inhale the bewitching scent of the floral displays.

As she moved her silken hair briefly covered her face and, when she straightened up again, he couldn't have been more surprised to see tears in her eyes.

'I know I'm being silly,' she said, facing him, 'but no one has ever done anything like this for me before, and I wish—'

She stopped and turned away.

Walking up to her, he put his hands lightly on her upper arms and, standing behind her, he stared out as she was doing across the flat oasis.

'You wish your mother could see it,' he whispered.

'You know?' She blinked the tears away and stared at him. Then she must have remembered what he'd said to her in the library about receiving information regarding her from the university.

'Of course your people will have researched every tiny detail regarding those you would meet,' she murmured, frowning a little.

'You must miss your mother.'

'Oh, yes…so much,' she admitted.

Isla wasn't sure how long they stood together in silence. She only knew, as emotion ravaged her, that Shazim seemed to understand her grief. She was angry with herself for showing him any weakness, but sometimes the grief she felt at her mother's passing was hard to hide. And then, confusingly, there was happiness too, knowing she had fulfilled her mother's dying wish by going back to university to continue her studies. She couldn't let her mother down now, but if she failed to meet her expectations in any way, she would.

And then there was also a totally unrealistic yearning for Shazim to put his arms around her, and she had to tell herself to stop wanting things she couldn't have. All this heart-searching would only distract her from her true purpose…

'Shall we eat?' he suggested.

The distraction of such a down-to-earth suggestion was a relief. She had opened her heart for a moment, showing him her true mixed-up feelings, and she could only be glad that he didn't pity her. He felt her sadness, and had recognized it as his own. In that they did share a bond. Perhaps they were coming to understand each other a little.

'I'd love to eat—I'm starving,' she said, turning around. Her heart leapt as Shazim smiled into her eyes at this sign of her spirit returning. 'Everything looks so delicious.'

'My team has worked hard,' he agreed. 'We mustn't disappoint them.'

Shazim put her at her ease. They sat side by side, but not touching each other, on cushions overlooking the oasis. It was only as the night progressed that Isla began to realize that what at first had appeared completely empty was in fact full of life... Birds silently skimmed the surface, while bats cavorted overhead. Fish leapt, their scales iridescent in the moonlight, while fireflies hovered like tiny dots of light against the darkness. There was a whole busy world, just waiting to be explored.

'This is the most beautiful place I've ever seen,' she told Shazim.

While she was still trying to get her head

around eating supper with a sheikh in such fabulous surroundings, they ate and talked at a leisurely pace.

Isla had been right in waiting, as she had put it, until they had something worthwhile to say. She'd done her homework on Q'Aqabi, and forced him to revisit details he hadn't considered for years. He had wanted to blot out so much of it, that now he could only be glad that she had prompted his recollections, and that they were as vivid as they had always been.

'And now you've got to show me the desert,' she insisted. 'I want to see it through your eyes—'

Her eyes were avid with eagerness, but his tone was sharp. 'No.'

She had asked him the one thing he could not do, and recoiled with surprise at his response.

'I have excellent rangers—the best in their field,' he explained to soften the blow. 'They will show you everything you should see.'

It took Isla a few moments to recover. She was clearly baffled and embarrassed by his sudden change of manner. When she spoke again she had changed too. She was circumspect, and almost reverential to the point where he could have roared with frustration. He didn't want reverence from Isla. He wanted her honesty and the frank and easy way in which she had previously spoken her mind to him.

'I apologise, Your Majesty. I realise that you must have far more important things to do than show me around.'

Nothing could be further from the truth. What could be more important than visiting the project that would have meant so much to his brother? He had hired the best brains, the best rangers, and the best equipment. Money was no object to him, and no effort had been spared. He had sat up late into the night for years, discussing the best outcome for each stage of the scheme with acknowledged experts in the field.

But had he seen the results of that endeavour first hand?

Wasn't it time to face his demons and go back into the desert?

Had this extraordinary woman pointed out the one flaw in his plan? Had she shown him in a single night that a scheme without a beating heart was doomed to fail—that it wouldn't inspire, it couldn't thrive, it couldn't last?

Springing to his feet, he stared down at her. 'I'll have the appropriate items you will need for your journey into the desert delivered to your suite. I will be ready and waiting to leave at dawn tomorrow morning.' And with that he strode away, leaving her staring after him in surprise.

* * *

After a restless night, tossing and turning as she wondered if she had insulted Shazim, Isla was up before dawn. She was excited at the prospect of visiting the desert, *and with him*, and a little apprehensive too. All her knowledge and understanding came from books. Would she be equal to the task when she faced reality?

Shazim offered no reassurance. When she joined him at the foot of the palace steps, she doubted she had ever seen him so grim and intent, or so remote from her before. Something had rattled him. Was it her? Dressed down in jeans and a figure-hugging top, with the polarised aviators pilots favoured shoved back on his thick black hair, Shazim looked more like a stuntman in a movie than a hard man of the desert. He was too good-looking to be real, but then appearances could be deceptive, and from everything she'd seen and heard about him Shazim was tempered steel.

They took an elevator to the roof of the palace where a squat black helicopter was waiting. She had never flown in a helicopter before, and had to admit to a flutter of nerves. It was only Shazim's air of command that calmed her enough to climb in. He was piloting the aircraft, and she tried not to look at the floor as he strapped her in. She'd had no idea it was see-through, but, of course, that made sense, though it wouldn't pay to have a fear of heights.

Having organised her headset and her microphone, Shazim made some last-minute checks and spoke to air traffic control. Seated next to him, she could see everything, and his confidence helped her to conquer her nerves as they lifted off. She relaxed to the point where she could enjoy the view…and not just the desert that stretched like an endless sea all around them, but the man at her side. He was like a rock beside her, powerful, certain, and calm. His shoulders had the span of a warrior's shoulders, but he was the protector of his people…and his lean, tanned hands, hands that had been so gentle on her arms last night, made her long to be in his embrace. She wanted to know everything about him—what made him sad, happy, and what made him smile. She had never felt like this about a man before and, after her experience at the hands of her attacker, she'd never thought she'd be able. She was sensible, practical, and competent. She had her fantasies, but had never considered bringing those fantasies into her life before.

Having Isla at his side and in his head was like salve on an open wound. He might have put off this trip for ever without her. Revisiting the desert was a pilgrimage for him. He owed it to his

brother to bring Isla and her new ideas to the
project. That was what had driven him here, and
now his hunger was growing to have the hands-
on role he had denied himself for too long. As
their shadow crept over the desert he was impatient to be down on the ground. He wanted
to feel the sand beneath his desert boots again.
He'd want Isla on his team, regardless of whether
or not he wanted her in his bed. She was loyal
and she was tough, and she wasn't fazed by anything…least of all him. She had stood up to him
every step of the way, and was strong-minded,
always doing what she believed to be right.

Too strong-minded, possibly?

He smiled a little. He liked the challenge she
gave him.

He glanced at Isla. She gave him a guarded
smile, but he could sense her excitement. She
was about to visit the nature reserve she had been
dreaming about. Checking in with flight control,
he signalled his intention to land.

'Oh,' she exclaimed, clinging onto her seat as
he swooped lower. 'Are we landing?'

'Yes.' He made a mental note not to fly as he
usually did, but to have some concern for his
passenger. He had grown tense at the thought of
revisiting the site of the tragedy, and was flying
on the edge of what was possible.

He shouldn't even be thinking about a woman

who could only be the briefest of distractions in his life when he had so much more to accomplish, he told himself firmly as he landed the bird.

The briefest of distractions?

Was that why he had dispatched his security team to watch over Isla when she had left the club in London? This was a woman who had revitalised him like a bolt of lightning to his core. She had shaken up his life when he had thought everything would be at an emotional standstill for ever. She'd made him see things differently, to the point where he knew now that Isla wouldn't be seeing the desert through his eyes, but he would be seeing this land he had once loved so deeply through hers.

CHAPTER SEVEN

ISLA WAS A child of nature, drawn to new experiences and adventure, as he had been as a youth. They had barely landed when she asked if she could visit the clinic. The Jeep was waiting for them, so he drove her there. He had barely switched off the engine when she crammed her hat onto her head and leapt out to brave the sun. It amused him to think that, for once, he wasn't taking the lead; nor was he the greater attraction. He followed her into the building, where he watched her take stock. He didn't need to introduce her; she'd already done that herself. He stayed just long enough to watch her roll up her sleeves and get to work.

She was still at the clinic three hours later working alongside his rangers. He knew they'd be grateful for her expertise. He was at the coral, where animals awaiting release into the wild were housed. A stab of very masculine jealousy hit him as he worked alongside his men. His rangers were all tough, good-looking guys, and Isla had brought grown men slavering to their knees at the pole-dancing club. His warrior genes had detonated at the sight of them devouring her with their eyes, though she'd handled them all with the same cool aplomb—handled him the same way. Even when she'd discovered who he was, it had made no difference to Isla.

Isla Sinclair. Warrior woman. The thought made him smile. He admired her guts, and her sheer, stubborn determination to do the work she loved, and to help those around her. Even at the club, the manager had told him how Isla had stepped in last minute to help a friend, and had been such a sensation that he wanted to offer her a job. Shazim had killed that idea, and for no reason he could fathom at the time—just gut instinct that told him there was some vulnerability beneath Isla's can-do attitude. He didn't know the root of it, but wouldn't countenance other men taking advantage of her—

'Your Majesty? Is everything all right?'

Seeing the expression on the rangers' faces, he realised how grim he'd become and had to clear thoughts of Isla from his mind. With a brief dip of his head, he said nothing as they walked past the spot he had avoided for so many years. The precipitous ledge where his life had changed for ever was part of the reserve. It was the heart of it. He would never avoid it again.

The desert was working its magic on him too, he mused as he stopped to stare around. Could Isla resist the magic? Anticipation roared through him at the thought of finding out.

Her first experience of the real desert did not disappoint in any way. The palace had been fabulous, and the extraordinary new experiences in a place of such opulence and craftsmanship had been a real eye-opener for her, but this wild, dangerous place was where Isla knew she belonged. And though her dreams had been mini-adventures, nothing could have prepared her for this reality. The immensity of the landscape, and the great bowl of electric-blue sky arcing over the seemingly boundless ocean of sand, made her feel very small and very insignificant, but, oh-so eager to begin. She loved the clinic, and the rangers, and the animals. She slotted right in, and had never been happier in her work.

She stayed long after everyone else had left, and when she walked outside, it was twilight. The colours of the darkening sky were extraordinary, and she took a moment to give thanks for where she was. Purple, pewter, pink and aquamarine vied for supremacy, filling her with a sense of happiness, a sense of belonging. Stretching out her arms to touch the air, she shook them to loosen her muscles. She needed it after concentrated working for so long. There was only one thing missing now, she reasoned wryly, and that was Shazim, though she doubted he would have time for her. Her assistants had told her that he had taken another group of rangers deeper into the desert, so he could observe the progress of the latest animal release programme.

Isla's imagination was only too eager to supply romantic images for this. Shazim would be dressed in flowing robes, and seated on a prancing stallion as he stood for a moment silhouetted against a darkening sky.

When he actually arrived, it was in a convertible Jeep, and he was wearing the same jeans and top he'd been wearing all day. Shazim was driving, and the group of rangers with him looked tired but happy, while Shazim looked more alive than she had ever seen him. His fierce stare sought out hers immediately, and when the rangers went their own way he came up to her.

'What?' he asked, no doubt seeing the bemused look on her face. 'Were you picturing a desert sheikh dressed in flowing robes, with a *howlis* wrapped around his head, riding towards you through a shimmering heat haze?'

'At night?' she said, curving the suspicion of a smile.

'Perhaps there was a prancing stallion involved,' he suggested with more than a suspicion of irony.

'In fact, there was,' she said, blunt as ever. She was glad of the new ease between them, and didn't want to do anything to put a spoke in that.

'So how did I look?' he asked.

She shrugged. 'Pretty good, considering there's no prancing stallion in the mix.'

He smiled. 'Only pretty good?'

She felt the heat of Shazim's smile in every part of her body as they walked side by side, back to the clinic.

'Anyway, welcome again to Q'Aqabi,' he said as he opened the door. 'I hope your first working day went well?'

'I couldn't have asked for more,' she said honestly.

Breath hitched in her throat as Shazim paid her the compliment of the traditional Q'Aqabian greeting, touching his forehead, his lips and then his heart. 'I hope you will be very happy here, Isla Sinclair.'

For the first time, she felt like curtseying to him, but a shiver of arousal soon chased that thought away, and she confined herself to a circumspect response. 'Thank you, Your Majesty.'

'Shazim,' he reminded her, fixing his stare on hers.

'Shazim,' she repeated softly, thinking his eyes

were as deep and dark as the ocean—and her heart was going crazy.

If Shazim had been attractive before, he was a devastating distraction in the desert. He seemed more primal here, and his power was undeniable in a land where physical strength and understanding of the wilderness could save lives.

She also knew what she was doing, Isla reassured herself. She might not know the desert as well as Shazim, but she was confident in her ability, and in her common sense, and all she asked for was to be a small but vital cog in the engine that drove Shazim's conservation project.

'Well,' she said when he closed the door behind them. 'What now? Are we heading back to the palace?'

'Not yet.'

A ripple of alarm attacked her, until Shazim explained. 'Now we relax, swim, celebrate—there's a village nearby where a new underground spring has been discovered. I thought you'd like to come with me and join in the celebrations. You'd be meeting some of the people you'd be working for. This is their land. We are only their servants, and you should meet them.'

'Of course.' She was eager to meet the local people...though the thought of going deeper into the wilderness with Shazim was daunting.

* * *

'Oh, no—I don't ride,' Isla protested when they went outside to find that one of the rangers had brought up two horses.

'You must ride. You have to for this trip,' Shazim insisted. 'It's the quickest way for us to reach the village.'

His reproving stare acted like a firm hand moving slowly across her body, until the desire to see more of the desert with Shazim became an irresistible urge.

'You'll need some suitable headgear,' he said, staring with a frown at her safari hat.

Before she'd had chance to refuse, he had deftly wound a long scarf around her face and neck.

'No more excuses,' he commanded. 'Mount up.'

She could do this, Isla told herself firmly as she eyed up the horse with suspicion. The horse eyed her back with matching suspicion. She loved animals. She loved being able to help them when they were sick, and seeing them recover best of all, but could she, who had never ridden a horse in her life before, ride through the desert alongside a sheikh, who was about to spring onto the back of the prancing stallion of her dreams?

'What are you waiting for?' Shazim prompted.

She sucked in a shocked breath as he put his

big hand over hers, but he was only showing her how to hold the reins. He guided her other hand to the pommel of the saddle, and now his big frame was just a breath away. Her entire body was trembling. If she made the smallest movement she would touch him.

'Put your foot in my hand,' he instructed, marshalling her straying thoughts. 'I'm going to lift you, and then you must settle gently onto the saddle.'

She was anxious, and the horse knew it. She got there somehow, and used every muscle she possessed to ensure she didn't land heavily in the saddle. But now she was too high off the ground.

'This isn't going to work,' she exclaimed. 'He knows I'm nervous.'

'Then, your only option is to ride in front of me,' Shazim instructed curtly as he picked up his reins.

She only had to take one look at his warhorse to change her mind. 'I'll manage,' she said grimly.

'Better not—'

She yelped as he lifted her off the saddle, and lowered her onto the saddle in front of him. She barely had chance to open her mouth to protest before the stallion lunged forward. And then it was too late. She was pressed up hard against Shazim, and they were moving as one. A shuddering breath shot out of her body as she registered every hard muscle in his powerful frame—

Shazim was a sheikh, the ruler of this land, and she worked for him. There was no romance. There were no billowing tents, no sandy shores of an oasis, no silken cushions, or pierced brass lanterns casting a honeyed light, waiting for her. There was just hard work, and the joy she always found in helping animals. She must keeping reminding herself of this… She was *not* here to lose her head—and heart—to a sheikh!

'I can't understand that you've never learned to ride,' Shazim said, frowning as he eased the powerful animal into a rolling canter.

It was a moment before she could reply. She was scared, she was thrilled—who wouldn't be? She was on the back of a mighty horse in the arms of a powerful sheikh.

'Why would I learn to ride?' she managed at last on a tight throat. She was still getting used to the unaccustomed gait. 'You live in a different world from me. You ride for necessity, while I take a bus. I've done plenty of fantasy riding as a little girl, but never in the arms of a sheikh—'

He laughed. 'You need to relax,' he said, binding her even closer.

And how was she supposed to do that?

It was only one small step from growing tense again, to wondering if fate had thrown them together for a purpose, and she had to remind herself yet again that she was a hard-working vet, while Shazim was a king, and master of all he surveyed. When her time in Q'Aqabi was done, she'd go home and he would stay here. There was no point wondering where the Lion of the Desert was taking her, or what they'd do when they arrived.

He should have left Isla to travel with his rangers. He was enjoying this too much. He had wanted her to share this special moment of triumph with his people, to help her understand the country she was here to help.

He moved her hand away when Isla tried to collect her hair and tie it back. Her scarf had flown off, and she was concerned that she didn't lash him in the face with it. But seeing that glorious hair flying behind her like a banner was all the impetus he needed to urge his stallion on. He leaned forward and she leaned with him, making the temptation to brush her hair aside and kiss her neck overwhelming.

CHAPTER EIGHT

HE WAS PRESSED up hard against her when Isla caught her first sight of the village lights twinkling in the distance. Her face lit up the night as she swung around to exclaim, 'Oh, Shazim, it's so beautiful!'

And so was she, he thought, though the glow of pleasure on Isla's face only emphasised her innocence, which made her seem more vulnerable than ever.

'And there's an oasis!' she said with excitement.

'Of course. All settlements are sited close to water—'

'Which is why they're so scarce in the desert,' she added.

Her excitement touched him. He had never noticed how beautiful her pure energy was before. It went beyond the physical to something that shone in her eyes. Seeing everything through those eyes was like seeing it for the first time for him.

'Look, Shazim...' She pointed out across the oasis. 'The water's so smooth, it's like a silken veil covered in spangles of moonlight.'

He smiled at her romantic description but quickly forced his mind back to practicalities. 'Put your scarf back,' he said. 'There's a wind kicking up, and you don't want to get your hair all clogged with grit and dust.'

'Thank you,' she said as he helped her to arrange the folds of cloth. Her voice on his skin was like a soft caress.

The touch of Shazim's hand on her neck had made her quiver with arousal and she could only hope he hadn't noticed. She didn't want to do anything that could be misinterpreted by him, or that might threaten their professional working relationship. She didn't want to do anything to spoil this perfect night—

Don't feel too guilty, her inner cynic warned her, *because perfect doesn't last...*

'People have come from miles around,' Shazim explained, distracting her from this troubling thought. As they drew closer to the village she could see how many campfires were studding the darkness with pinpoints of light, and she thrilled at the thought of meeting his people, but it was Shazim's breath, warm on her neck, that made her body thrill.

'Are you cold?' he asked as she shivered with awareness of him.

'I'm excited,' she answered with a healthy dose of truth. 'I'm excited to see something so new to me, and to join in the celebrations.'

'Don't worry,' Shazim assured her in the deep, husky voice that made her tremble again. 'You'll be safe with me.'

Would she? Was Shazim a safe haven, or was he a dangerous destination for a woman who knew so little about love?

Love?

Sex, Isla conceded ruefully. She knew so little about sex. Shazim, on the other hand, was a totem to physicality, and she doubted there was much he didn't know.

So...would she be safe?

She'd only find that out when she got there.

'I'm happy for you—' She turned to flash a look into Shazim's heavily shadowed face, and felt another thrill of awareness. 'I'm happy for Q'Aqabi, and for your people. I know what this latest discovery of a new water supply must mean to everyone.'

He hummed in reply, and the vibration of that sound transferred from his body to hers.

News of the important discovery had spread like wildfire, and the city of tents made the small village appear to sprawl for miles. The sound of music and laughter, and conversation, constantly rose and fell like the murmur of surf on a distant shore.

'Dreaming again, Isla?' Shazim prompted as she sighed.

Realising that she'd leaned back against his chest to enjoy the moment, she huffed a smile and pulled away again fast. 'I'm a very practical woman,' she argued. 'You must know that by now.'

'Should I? And does your practical nature mean that you are forbidden to dream?'

There was humour in Shazim's voice, and his comment raised a flutter of alarm. It was as if he had a window into her mind.

'What was your childhood like, Isla?'

She tensed at the unexpected question.

'Relax,' Shazim insisted. 'The stallion has to tackle a steep incline, and he doesn't need you tensing up, making it harder for him.'

No. Only his master was allowed to do that.

'Didn't your investigators tell you everything about me?' she queried, hoping the question would let her off the hook.

'Bare facts only,' Shazim said. She felt him shrug. 'I receive a briefing for everyone I'm likely to meet on a tour.'

So he was unlikely to know more than those bare facts about her, which was a relief. She didn't want to think back to the time Shazim was asking about, and remained silent as his horse picked a path down the dune.

'Everyone has a story to tell that goes beyond a cold-blooded report,' Shazim elaborated once they reached safe ground. 'I'd like to hear yours.'

'Well, I don't know anything about you,' she defended, then realised that she had definitely overstepped the mark. She could tell by the way Shazim had tensed. It wasn't her place to interrogate him, but as her employer he had the right to know more than those plain facts he had mentioned.

She wasn't the only one with pain in her past, and that should make her more understanding, not less. 'I was an only child, studious and serious,' she began. 'I'm sure you're surprised to hear that,' she teased, trying to make light of it. 'I read a lot.'

'And cultivated a vivid inner life thanks to your reading, I imagine?' Shazim suggested.

She smiled. 'I wouldn't deny that. I certainly had a vivid imagination. I still do. I've read that many only children have a lively inner life to take the place of all the adventures they might have had with their siblings—'

Shazim cut her off. 'What about your father? You never mention him.'

A chill ran through her at Shazim's prompt. 'I

can hardly remember him,' she said truthfully. Having successfully shut out the beatings and her mother's screams, the best she could come up with was, 'He left when I was very small. There was never another man in my mother's life.' It wouldn't have helped to add that the police took her father away, or that he was later locked up for assaulting several other women.

'And then, while you were studying at university, your mother became sick.'

'Long before that, but the illness became critical when I went away.'

'So you came back.'

'I broke off my studies, yes.'

'Though they mean so much to you,' Shazim prompted.

'Nothing meant more to me than my mother.'

His eyes clouded briefly as if he understood. Some had said her mother's illness and premature death had been the result of the years of cruelty at Isla's father's hands. Isla could never think back without wishing she could have taken on her mother's pain.

Shazim waited until she was ready to continue, and then he said, 'I apologise if my bringing up the past upsets you.'

His voice was gentler than before, but he had opened a wound that had never properly healed.

'Why do you want to know these things?' She sounded defensive.

'I'm interested in the welfare of everyone on my team. Do you find that so strange?'

'No,' Isla admitted. And it was up to her to handle the emotional fallout. It wasn't Shazim's fault that his questions had cut so deep. 'My mother was sick for most of my childhood. As I grew older, her illness progressed—'

'Until you became her full-time carer,' Shazim supplied when words choked off in her throat. 'You nursed her selflessly until the day she died, and gave up your education to do so.'

'Gladly.' Isla flared up as remembered pain lanced through her. 'Because I loved her—love her,' she amended passionately.

It was a relief when Shazim didn't attempt to shower her with sympathy, and simply stayed quiet until she spoke again. 'It was a bad time,' she admitted then, and with a considerable understatement.

'Yet you pulled yourself together and went back to university.'

'It was my mother's dearest wish. She insisted that I must.'

'She must have been a wonderful woman.'

'She was.'

'She would be very proud of you,' he said quietly.

'Thank you.'

They rode on in silence after that, with the simple village growing ever closer, until he said, 'And you grew up in a castle.'

'Not exactly inside the castle—that was a cold, unfriendly place. Not like this village,' she added as the warmth and music from the celebration washed over them. She only had to think back to the years of debauchery at the castle to know that this simple life had to be better. 'My mother was the cook at the castle,' she explained, 'though I suppose that's another fact you already know.'

'It's good to hear your side of things,' Shazim said. He had slowed the stallion to a lazy walk and had let his reins hang loose, as if he really wanted to hear her side of the story, and was making time to do so before they entered the village. 'All I know is that you were raised in the grounds of a castle in Scotland, alongside a family that could politely be called eccentric.' He gave an easy shrug. 'Who wouldn't be interested in that?'

'The Anconners held drug-fuelled parties,' Isla stated bluntly. 'I suppose you've heard that too. They cared nothing for their reputation, or for that of their staff. My mother stayed on out of a misplaced sense of loyalty, and we lived in a staff cottage on the estate.'

'But you had to leave—I don't understand. Why was that?'

Isla was silent for quite a while as she thought back. Shazim's grip tightened around her waist as if he wanted to reassure her. 'We left the cottage when my mother became too ill to work,' she explained. 'We had to,' she said when Shazim gave a jerk of surprise.

'You *had* to?' he said in a bemused tone.

'If my mother couldn't work, we had no place at the castle.'

'Is that why you moved into the room where you still live now?'

'Yes.' She didn't want to talk about it. It hurt too much to think of her mother uprooted when she had needed the familiarity of her own home the most.

But Shazim refused to let it go. 'One room must have been a bit of a comedown after a castle?'

'We made it home. It was our home, and we were safe there. No one was going to throw us out.' Her voice reflected her emotion as she remembered the tiny room that she had shared with her mother in the last days of her mother's life.

Isla had made it safe, Shazim concluded. Isla had protected her mother like a lioness with a cub, reversing their positions when it became necessary—the cared for becoming the carer in her mother's hour of need.

'I loved our cottage on the castle estate,' she murmured wistfully. 'It wasn't much, but it was home—my mother made it home, so I did the same when we moved into that room. We didn't have anything much, but the funny thing is I don't remember going without anything. We were warm and safe...'

'But you missed the cottage,' he pressed when she became silent.

'Nothing could match that,' Isla admitted. 'I was born in the cottage, and I lived there all my life. It never once occurred to me that I wouldn't be able to always call the cottage home.'

'That's how it should have been,' Shazim insisted. 'I can't believe you didn't have a right to tenancy after living in the cottage for so many years?'

'We couldn't have afforded it, and Lady Anconner explained quite clearly to me that the cottage went with the job.'

'When did she tell you this?'

'Lady Anconner visited us after my mother's first hospital admission. I was so thrilled for my mother when her ladyship knocked on the door, but I was puzzled too—Lady Anconner wasn't exactly noted for her kindness, though I knew my mother would appreciate the gesture.'

'And did she?' he quizzed.

'My mother was so excited to be remembered by the people from the big house that she wouldn't hear a word against her ladyship—even when Lady Anconner explained that if my mother could no longer cook for them, then we would have to leave the cottage so they could hire someone else, and that someone else would live there instead of us.'

He was appalled. 'She threw you out, knowing your mother was so ill?'

'It was pure economics—at least, that's what Lady Anconner said, and my mother agreed with her. She said that was how things had always been at the castle.'

'And this so-called lady couldn't change the status quo for someone who was desperately ill, and who had lived in the cottage all her working life?'

'Lady Anconner didn't want to—she couldn't, really. All those colourful stories you've heard about the Anconner parties were true. How could they host them without staff to wait on their guests?'

They could have tidied up one of the unused attic rooms for a new member of staff to use, and left a dying woman in the only home she'd ever known. That was what he thought, but he kept his feelings to himself. High passion was too little too late, and it wouldn't help Isla.

'I hear the Anconners are bankrupt now,' he said instead.

Isla eased her shoulder in a hesitant shrug before answering, and then she said, 'I haven't really had time to follow their story.'

He doubted that was true, but he let it go. There was too much hurt in Isla's voice, and that hurt was as fresh as the day Lady Anconner had shattered her mother's dreams. How anyone could be so cold-hearted was beyond him. However aristocratic this Lady Anconner might think herself, in his view she had no claim to the title 'lady'.

'You grew up in a royal nursery,' Isla reminded him, jolting him out of his preoccupation with her past. 'That couldn't have been easy for you—being distanced from your parents?'

'I had siblings,' he said thinking back. 'And my elder brother was like a father to us.'

'And now?' she prompted softly as if she knew she was treading on hallowed ground.

He ignored the question, and turned instead to a subject of his choosing. Looking around at the crowds gathering in the tented city, he commented, 'Mixing with my people was always a joy to me.'

'Have you been spending too much time in your ivory tower, Shazim?'

He laughed, and shook his head at Isla's disrespect. 'Too much time looking at schedules, balance sheets, and architects' drawings,' he admitted.

'Someone has to do it.'

'Are you making excuses for me, Ms Sinclair?' He leaned forward to murmur this in her ear, and felt her quiver with awareness. The connection between them pleased him. He'd never experienced it with anyone before, and was grateful to Isla for bringing him down to earth and reminding him that he was in danger of forgetting where he came from, and who he was.

'Shazim?' she prompted when he fell silent.

'Tell me more about your life,' he insisted, keen to swerve the spotlight from himself.

She didn't want to talk about her past, and closed her eyes to shut it out. She didn't want to remember the humiliation of a little girl, forbidden entrance to the castle where her mother was working, or being shooed away like an untrustworthy urchin, who wasn't even good enough to enter by the back door. And though the two things weren't connected, she certainly didn't want to remember what had made her so wary of men.

'Thanks to my mother I had the best of childhoods,' she insisted, glossing over the more unpalatable facts. 'We got through just fine.' That was a lie too, but how would it help her mother now, if Isla dwelled on all the comforts she hadn't been able to give her mother?

'The castle is up for sale, I hear,' Shazim prompted.

He said this without expression, but she was wary. 'I hope you're not thinking of buying it. It was such an unhappy place.'

'If I do, I'll raze it to the ground,' he promised harshly. 'My world is here in Q'Aqabi, with my people, and my projects.' He paused for a moment, and then said, 'You've done really well in achieving what you have, Isla.'

'As have you,' she said with her usual forthrightness.

'We do share some similarities,' he conceded on a laugh. 'Trust you to point them out to me.'

'I just follow my heart,' she admitted.

'And has your heart never led you astray?'

Isla fell silent. She didn't speak again until they arrived in the village.

CHAPTER NINE

THE VILLAGERS CLUSTERED around Shazim's stallion. News of the Sheikh of Q'Aqabi's arrival had quickly spread, and a great crowd followed them into the village. What they made of the woman seated in front of the Lion of the Desert remained to be seen. Shazim didn't appear to be remotely concerned, but Isla was. Her only experience of wealth and privilege had not been a good one, and this event, thrilling though it was, was a stark reminder of the power Shazim wielded. Coupled with his immense wealth, it left her at an extreme disadvantage. She had almost relaxed with him during their ride through the desert, but now she was growing tense again.

He had become acutely conscious of Isla's smallest reaction while they were pressed up close on the horse. He would have had to be asleep not to register every nuance in her body language, and he had felt Isla shrink defensively into herself as people stared at them. He guessed that this was partly because he had prompted her to talk about her unhappy childhood, when she had been belittled and humiliated by people who should have known better. She had certainly felt awkward riding into the village in front of him, and probably thought his people would be critical of her, when he knew they would welcome her as a guest of their Sheikh. His people would have been more surprised if he'd kept such a beautiful woman away from them. Isla was different, special, he reflected, scanning her slender shoulders and the tumble of hair that had escaped her scarf, and they would see that, as he did.

Would bedding Isla ease her tension? Maybe, but he wanted more of her than a single night, and could he risk indulging himself and potentially losing a valuable member of his team? Isla might be newly qualified, but she had an outstanding record at the university, and he would be risking all she was on the altar of lust.

Those were his virtuous thoughts, but another part of him wanted to take Isla's softly yielding body and awaken her to pleasure.

'You're very quiet,' she said.

'I was enjoying the silence,' he commented drily.

'Oh, I see,' she said, responding to his mocking tone. 'You should maybe have left me behind if you wanted silence.'

He hummed in agreement. He needed a distraction fast. Isla was soft and pliant against him, and her hair was fragrant against his lips. Her wildflower scent was intoxicating—there was just one problem. He had never ridden a horse with such a painful erection before.

The crowd followed them to a recently erected pavilion reserved for their King. It soon became evident that in honour of his visit the vast tent had been sited directly over the new water source in the shadow of a towering cliff. The pavilion was quite private. Clustering palms and the discretion of the villagers would make sure of it.

Isla was impressed. If this wasn't quite the billowing Bedouin tent of her fantasies, it was close. Maybe it was even a little better than her fantasy with the Sheikh's personal pennant flying from the topmost point. The flag, with its ground of cerulean blue, bore a lion rampant in gold with crimson claws. A shiver tracked down her spine as she stared at the rearing lion, towering over its helpless prey.

Yes. Well. She wasn't exactly helpless, and she wasn't about to become anyone's prey.

Shazim's royal house...his royal privilege... his castle...

She had to close her eyes and close her mind to the feelings from the past that threatened to intrude now and spoil everything.

'The pavilion is yours to use as you wish,' Shazim said, distracting her as he reined in his stallion.

'Mine?' she queried with surprise.

'I'm going to greet my people, and then I'm going for a swim before the festivities begin,' Shazim announced as he sprang down to the ground.

'But I thought you were sleeping here?' she said as he reached up to her.

'I'll find somewhere else. Take it,' he said impatiently. 'It's yours for the night.'

Scientist or not, she couldn't help but feel rejected, with her fantasies lying flat on the ground. 'If you're sure?' she said, dismounting carefully so she wouldn't join them.

'I'm sure,' Shazim insisted, holding the big horse steady as she got off.

It had looked so easy when Shazim sprang down that she launched herself into thin air with every confidence that she would land safely on her feet. Unfortunately, that didn't go too well, and as the stallion pawed the ground with the same impatience as his master she was thrown off balance. She would have landed on her face if Shazim hadn't reached out to catch hold of her. He steadied her, but now her muscles protested after so much unaccustomed horseback riding, and she stumbled, almost falling to her knees, forcing him to catch hold of her again.

'You'll get used to it.' His black eyes were burning with amusement.

'Will I?' She gave him a hard stare, which failed to counteract the feelings flooding through her as Shazim held her safe in his arms.

'I guarantee it,' he murmured. 'Meanwhile, I suggest a massage.'

'What I need is a hot bath.' She flared up as all her old fears regarding men came back to haunt her. Then, realising what she'd said, and how insensitive it must have sounded when water was such a precious commodity in the desert, even more valuable than oil, she added, shamefaced, 'Forgive me. I do know how thoughtless that must have sounded.'

'You can take as many baths as you want.' Shazim shrugged. 'This new water supply makes everything possible. In fact, I'll order water to be drawn for your bath right away.'

'Please—no. I'm perfectly capable of doing that myself. I don't want anyone going to any trouble on my behalf.' Though she did need Shazim to let her go right away before her senses went into permanent meltdown.

'Whatever you want,' he said with his face so close to hers, her cheeks tingled.

A pulse of something warm and seductive

throbbed inside her. It was definitely time for her to make her move—out of his arms. 'Thanks for the save,' she said matter-of-factly.

Testing her legs only proved that she wasn't ready to let go of him, and hanging onto Shazim was dynamite to her senses.

'Are you sure you can do without me?' he mocked her softly.

'Of course I can.' Letting go, she set off again, and this time managed to stagger a few steps. Shazim's expression as he watched her was both intimate and sexy. It warmed her. He warmed her, and in all sorts of dangerous ways.

They were employer and employee, Isla told herself sternly. She'd had a few flings with boys at school and university, but the Sheikh of Q'Aqabi was definitely not a boy. There had been no time for romance in her life while she was caring for her mother, and then she'd been too busy studying to get back into college as she'd promised her mother she would. After the near attack, she was grateful for the excuse to avoid relationships. She was an innocent throwing herself to the lion, while everything about Shazim suggested his experience of things like sex was beyond her comprehension.

'I think you'd better get that massage,' he suggested as she yelped and stumbled again. Before she could say no, he swung her into his arms.

And, pausing only to free the fastening on the tent flap so that it fell into place behind them, he carried her to a bed of silken cushions and laid her down. Straightening up, he turned to go. Pausing briefly by the entrance, he recommended, 'Take a bath and work those muscles.'

She'd been dumped—literally, like a sack of potatoes. Perversely, though, she hadn't wanted him to stay; Shazim being in such a hurry to leave had left her feeling plain and undesirable.

She'd got everything she deserved. She wasn't living out a fantasy. This was real life, with real aching legs. It would take time to work those muscles, and that was what she should do. She was no use to anyone until she could get about.

And it wouldn't help to imagine Shazim carrying out the massage...starting at her calves and working up. The faster she returned to full working order—and that meant her brain too—the sooner she could explore the village and see if there was anything in the veterinary line she could help out with.

As soon as she could she went exploring. She started with the pavilion, which was huge, and pleasantly shaded. It was faintly scented with some delicious spice, and packed full of craftsmanship. The colours were muted, and everything looked well loved, as if nothing was too much trouble for the people's Sheikh. The tent was full of ethnic treasures, many of which bore the patina of age, and should probably be housed in a museum, Isla mused, running her fingertips across the intricately carved surface of an ancient chest. And Shazim had given all this up for her.

The huge bed in the centre of the pavilion had been made ready for him. Dressed in white silk sheets, it was shaded by gossamer curtains. Alongside the bed there were low tables laden with jugs of juice, and bowls of fresh fruit—there was even a brass campaign bath, she saw now, full of warm, scented water. Hugging herself, she smiled as she glanced around. One option was stay here all night, and live the dream... The other was to go into the village to see if there was any work she could do.

'She's doing what?'

'Working, Your Majesty,' one of his rangers assured him.

Any pictures he might have conjured up of Isla waiting for him, soft and fragrant after her bath, could take a hike. Apparently, she had freshened up, and then taken a walk through the village to find the animal clinic. Having run a quick assessment of need, she had asked one of the rangers to show her where they kept their stock of medical supplies.

Isla couldn't be stopped. She was exceptional.

But this wasn't a work detail. On this occasion, she was his guest.

A regular guest, or a special guest?

Beneath her can-do ability, Isla was a green shoot waiting to be trampled. She deserved more than the cliché of a moonlit night with the desert Sheikh. Inevitably, she would be sidelined after serving his needs. He could offer her nothing. His duty was to his country. The debt he owed his late brother demanded nothing less of him. He wasn't totally without heart. He would make Isla's time in Q'Aqabi enjoyable—if she stopped working long enough for him to do so.

A glint of amusement flared in his eyes when he found her. Brow pleated, lips firmed, she was intent on her work. The challenge of distracting her was something he looked forward to.

'The celebrations?' he reminded her.

She glanced up. Her cheeks pinked and her eyes darkened as she stared at him. Betraying more than she cared to, he suspected.

'Just a few more minutes and I'll be done,' she said.

He shrugged and pulled away from the door. They were both driven. He could accept that, but she should chill out. One of them needed to.

The last thing Isla had expected when she returned from the clinic was that the women of the village would want to thank her for treating their family pets alongside those on the Sheikh's programme. Isla had thought nothing of offering her services, beyond the fact that all her patients were creatures in need, but now the women were offering to share their best clothes with her.

Staring down at her travel-worn outfit, she had to agree that a change of clothes was in order. The safari suit she was wearing had been recommended by an outdoor clothing store in England, and was way too hot and heavy for the desert. It had far too many pockets bulking it out, for one thing, even for someone who customarily carried a wound-suturing kit alongside her lip balm.

And she could do with another freshening up after her work in the clinic, Isla concluded as her new friends drizzled fragrant oil in the bath they had prepared for her. She only balked when they brought out coffers of family jewels for her to wear. She couldn't do that, she explained with mimes and gestures, as they were far too precious.

After bathing, they insisted on massaging scented oils into her skin, and then they dressed her in a delicately embroidered robe of floating silk chiffon in a soft peach shade. She had never worn anything quite so beautiful. Even the gown the maid had chosen for her at the palace hardly compared to this, for this was a lovingly preserved gown that had been passed down through the generations. She could see that in the tiny darns and repairs, which she believed made it more precious than the most expensive couture gown, for every stitch had been sewn with love.

So this was her second time in a flowing gown, when she could count the number of times she had worn a dress on the fingers of one hand. She'd always been a tomboy, rather than a girly girl, but this dream of a dress, beaded in silver and hung with tiny bells that sang as she walked, was more than enough to convert her. She felt like Cinderella dressing up for the ball.

Hadn't she sworn off Cinderella?

Anyone would make an exception for this gown, and she had no intention of offending the women of the village by refusing their kindness and generosity in lending it to her.

At the first touch of the cool silk gliding over her naked body, Isla wondered if the gown might be the key to holding Shazim's interest for longer than five minutes. There were things she wanted to talk to him about—improvements to the clinic, for instance.

For a moment, she forgot about work. The gown was transforming, and she turned full circle to show it off to the women, laughing with them as she stared at her reflection in the full-length mirror. She doubted she would ever get the chance to wear a gown like this again.

'You're very generous. Thank you…'

She went to each of the women in turn, smiling her thanks into their eyes. But they hadn't finished with her yet. Her hair had to be polished, and then scented before they placed a dramatic and very beautiful veil on her head. They left her hair loose beneath the veil, and pinned it in place with tiny jewelled pins. Even her hands and feet had to be softened with fragranced cream, and then they persuaded her to slip her feet into dainty sandals.

All good so far, but could she lose her tomboy strut?

As she watched the village women flitting around the pavilion like so many beautiful, graceful scented moths, Isla felt like a clumsy oaf. Perhaps this was all a dream, and she'd wake up to find that she was snoozing beneath a pile of bandages, or a page of notes.

When the women were finally satisfied with her appearance, they gathered around her so they could lead her to the celebration. She was thrilled, and also self-conscious. She'd done it once before, but that was just with Shazim at his palace. Could she pull off this new and very different identity in front of a crowd?

She'd played roles before, Isla reminded herself sensibly. In fact, she'd played so many roles they must have made Shazim's head spin. This was just one more.

Thoughts of her mother reassured her as the women led her out of the pavilion. Her mother would have loved to see Isla dressed like this. She had always tried to get her to wear pretty dresses when she was a little girl, and would have laughed with sheer joy to see her ragtag daughter dressed like the princess she had always wanted her to be.

She would hold her head up high and wring every drop of happiness out of each moment, Isla decided. It was a privilege to be here, and to be part of this celebration. That was the only way she knew to thank the women for all the trouble they'd gone to on her behalf, as they tried to make a silk purse out of a sow's ear, though what Shazim would think of their handiwork remained to be seen. Her heart gave a bounce as she thought about him.

A vast crowd had gathered in the centre of the village. The women led her forward towards the large bonfire in the centre that had been lit to ward off the chill of a desert night. Everyone was sitting cross-legged on cushions around Shazim, and every age group was represented. His audience was rapt, and she stopped walking for a moment to listen to him. She couldn't understand the language, but the tone of his voice affected her, and she found herself imagining how it might feel to have Shazim talk to her in that same profoundly caring way.

Nothing in her fantasies could compare with this, Isla decided as she looked around. There were camels instead of cars beneath the palm trees, and cicadas chirruped in the background as night owls swooped overhead. The air was warm and fragranced with wood smoke, while the fiery sky above her head was fading to magenta on its way to impenetrable inky black. She was beginning to understand what people meant when they talked about the magic of the desert. Q'Aqabi was a very special place, with special people, and a special man to rule over them. Shazim, she knew now, was both a force to be reckoned with, and a man to admire.

He startled her by looking up and staring directly at her. All her confidence drained away when he beckoned to her, but the women took hold of her hands and drew her forward to sit with their Sheikh.

CHAPTER TEN

THE CAMPFIRE SEEMED to blaze higher than ever as she approached. The hot light emphasised Shazim's chiselled cheekbones and his regal profile. The women backed away respectfully, and, though there was a crowd of hundreds surrounding them, for a few moments Isla felt that she was alone with Shazim. His stare, so dark and commanding, pierced hers, drawing her towards him, until with a gesture he pointed her towards the cushions at his side. She had to remind herself that this regal figure was the same man she had met in London on a building site, but here he seemed so much more. Like her, Shazim was dressed in traditional robes. His were night-blue silk, and the soft folds pressed insistently against his powerful frame. He might as well have been naked. She could all too easily imagine him naked, and swallowed deep. To have that huge, muscular body looming over her—

What was she thinking?

But it proved impossible to sit next to him without that idea flashing through her head.

She had sat down awkwardly. There wasn't much room and she was hampered by skirts. There was such a press of people around Shazim that she was pressed up hard against him. That was all it took for her to remember how it felt to be in his arms—though she had only been there by default—on his horse, and then when she'd tripped over. Imagining how it would feel to be in his arms, if it were planned, should not even make it into her wildest fantasy.

But it did. And she felt her cheeks flame when Shazim turned his attention to her. It didn't help when everyone fell silent to watch, and she could only be thankful that it was dark so her red cheeks were hidden from the villagers.

'I was just telling the elders of the village what an asset you are to our project,' Shazim explained.

She drew a sharp breath in. His words were innocent, but his gaze had drifted to her lips. 'I will do anything I can to help,' she heard herself say, staring at Shazim's mouth. She couldn't help but remember his chaste kisses on each cheek, only now she was wondering if they'd been quite as chaste as she had imagined.

'You are a very talented woman,' he said, directing this comment to the crowd, and then translating for them into Q'Aqabian. 'We want you to feel that you can spread your professional wings here—'

At his mention of her professional wings she was able to relax.

'Anything you need, I will see you have,' he said.

Again, his words were harmless on the surface, but there was something in Shazim's eyes that spoke of different needs, and different rewards for her compliance, and she grew instantly tense again when he added, 'Your every wish is my command, Ms Sinclair.'

Try as she might, she could not subdue the pleasure pulses that his words alone could produce, and when Shazim smiled into her eyes it was as if the great Sheikh of Q'Aqabi could read her mind.

Leaning towards her, he whispered so only she could hear, 'Don't look so worried. I'll keep you safe.'

Safe?

There was nothing safe about Shazim. She would be naive to think so. He might look like a figure from a fable: remote, and too principled to take advantage of this situation, but underneath he was just a man…a man whose head was uncovered, and whose thick black hair was unruly as it always was, and slightly damp, as if he'd been swimming in the oasis. Luxuriant inky waves had caught on his sharp black stubble, and as he smiled faintly there was intimacy and promise in his eyes; she knew he wasn't thinking of her veterinary skills.

'I approve of your outfit,' he said, lifting one brow. 'It's a great improvement on that ugly safari.'

'Though this is not as practical for working in the clinic,' she pointed out.

'True,' Shazim agreed with a dark look that made her senses soar. 'And your legs—'

'My legs?' she queried, and had to remind herself not to speak so loudly, as everyone had quietened again to listen.

'Are your legs recovered after your ride?' Shazim asked smoothly, and in a few moments, realising there was nothing wrong, people started chattering amongst themselves again.

'Like the rest of me, my legs are resilient,' she said, which made him laugh.

'I'm pleased to hear it. I intend to give them a lot of work while you're here.'

The look was back again, and she was still trying to fathom out how to handle Shazim in this mood when he turned to talk to the elder on his other side.

'Don't worry—'

She started as Shazim swung around and interrupted her. 'I've told everyone how much they can expect of you.'

'Ah,' she said as he turned away again. But what did Shazim expect of her?

Thanks to the press of people, his thigh had remained pressed against hers, and the contact between them was having all sorts of powerful effects on her body. She felt his heat, and the brush of his arm on her breast when he leaned across her to find her some delicacy to try was just too intimate.

She was about to get up, to see if there was somewhere else to sit, when he offered her a sweetmeat dripping with honey.

'No more, please,' she begged, not trusting herself to take it from his fingers.

She couldn't take much more of his sensual torture, and decided she must go to bed. She started to explain that she was tired after her journey, but Shazim's frown stopped her. 'The women have gone to so much trouble, and now you're going to bed?' he demanded.

Put that way, he did make her sound rude. She sat down again. She could hardly admit to Shazim that it was the survival of her professional identity troubling her now, and that he was the cause of her concern. But then, some of the women who'd helped her to dress looked across and smiled encouragement, and she knew she had to stay for them.

Experience burned in Shazim's eyes every time he looked at her, and, while she could be sensible, her body refused point-blank.

Entertainment after the banquet provided some distraction. This included horse riders performing incredible stunts, and there were fire-eaters, acrobats, and jugglers, as well as traditional dancers of both sexes. It was a wonderful evening and, in spite of all the troubling thoughts where Shazim was concerned, she could only thank her lucky stars that she was here.

Her heart leapt with fear when Shazim was challenged to ride a dangerous race, in which the riders were expected to snatch a flag before their opponents could reach it. Shazim didn't hesitate to join in, and called at once for his great stallion.

Wishing him good luck hardly seemed enough. Shazim was a great horseman, but he would be given no quarter here, no allowances for being a king. Every man was equal in the race.

She leapt to her feet and held her breath along with the rest of the crowd, as Shazim urged his mighty stallion forward. Just as the race was about to start a cloud covered the moon. A collective sigh went up, as if this was a portent of what was to come, and Isla's heart thudded as the sky turned black as ink.

Flambeaux were quickly lit to light the way, casting giant shadows across the sand. It was like watching a film, she thought as the cheers of the crowd became deafening. But this was all too real, and suddenly she was frightened for Shazim.

The flag went down and horses plunged forward. Riders risked everything, and there were too many, too close. She needn't have worried about Shazim, Isla saw with relief. Having taken an early lead, he was well ahead of the other riders, an advantage that allowed him to avoid the death-dealing jostle around the flag. A great cheer went up as he dipped low over the side of his horse to snatch the prize. Isla was weak with relief, though she was cheering with the rest when Shazim wheeled his stallion around so fast it reared up and, controlling it masterfully, he galloped back victorious, holding the flag on high.

Closing her eyes briefly, she sent up thanks to all the fates for keeping him safe, and when she opened them again Shazim was in front of her on his mighty stallion, which snorted and stamped as it eyed her imperiously.

'Take it,' he commanded, still high on the adrenaline of victory as he held out the flag.

She grasped the pole still warm from his hand

and, stretching as high as she could, she waved it above her head.

When Shazim turned to acknowledge the cheers of the crowd, she was exultant for him. He was a rock to his people, and a force for good that she was only just beginning to understand.

When the excitement had died down and they returned to their cushions, she felt that Shazim's triumph, and her small part of it, had changed their relationship in some small, but significant way. It was as if, by handing her the flag, he had made a public declaration of her importance to him. She knew that was only in the field of veterinary sciences, but still...

She was more aware of him than ever, and while Shazim appeared more interested in chatting to the man on his other side, his body seemed to be speaking to hers, and those messages didn't need an interpreter. They were intimate, and on the rare occasions when he did look at her there was new heat in Shazim's eyes.

When the evening drew to a close, and people started heading off to bed, she waited until Shazim was free for a moment so she could say goodnight to him. So many people wanted to speak to him that she had to stand in line, but it gave her chance to smile and thank everyone for such a wonderful evening. And then it was her turn to speak to His Majesty, the Sheikh.

'Thank you, Shazim. I can't remember ever having such a wonderful night. I'll never forget it. And you were great,' she added with a cheeky twinkle. 'Congratulations on your victory, Your Majesty.'

'Did you doubt me?' Shazim demanded. His stern face softened into a smile.

'Not for a moment,' Isla said honestly. 'You had the best horse,' she added with another cheeky look.

Throwing back his head, Shazim laughed. 'Trust you to pop my pompous balloon.'

'You're not pompous—you just take yourself a little too seriously at times.'

The look he gave her this time made her heart race.

'I'm glad you've enjoyed yourself, Ms Sinclair.'

Shazim's voice was dark and husky, and his tone was tinged with the humour that could always make her toes curl, if only because it was so rare, and seemed to be reserved for her, as if everything else in Shazim's life were deadly serious.

'I will escort you back to the pavilion,' he said.

'I'm fine. I know my way,' she said, brushing off Shazim's offer as politely as she could. She knew where her boundaries lay, and while sitting next to him at the celebration was one thing, having Shazim accompany her to the isolated pavilion was very different.

'I insist,' he commanded, indicating she should go ahead of him.

She couldn't cause a scene in front of hundreds of Shazim's loyal subjects.

'The desert has more dangers than you know,' he added, sending shock waves down her arm as he began to guide her through the crowd. 'Landmarks can be deceiving. The weather is unpredictable. Everything can change in seconds.'

'Between here and the pavilion?' she queried in her usual down-to-earth way.

Thinking to put some sensible distance between them, she now only succeeded in having Shazim place his hand in the small of her back to keep her on track.

'You'd be surprised,' he said, urging her on with fingers slightly spread. 'There are rumours of a sandstorm on the way.'

At this, she shook the random thoughts of pleasure out of her head and paid attention. 'Surely, we would have heard something—some warning on the radio?'

'There are signs that only those who are familiar with the desert can interpret.'

'For instance?' she pressed, trying to concentrate with sensation streaming from Shazim's hand to her core.

'That unexplained gust of wind tonight that

blew off your scarf? That warned me to be vigilant,' he explained.

A lot of people were leaving at the same time, and the crowd had become a jostling mass. Putting his other hand on her shoulder, Shazim guided her safely through. Everyone fell back for him, she noticed.

'Storms can creep up slowly,' he said, his grip sliding slowly down her arm, 'or they can roar in on a following wind—'

She gasped as he pulled her close when she almost drifted into a camel.

'If you should stray out of the village, even by chance, during one of these turbulent episodes, I might never find you again.'

'Would you care?'

'Of course.' There was humour in his voice. 'How would I ever explain that to the university?'

'Thanks,' she said drily. 'But wouldn't a tracker solve the problem?'

'I wish you luck with your tracker in a sandstorm.'

'All right,' she conceded as they turned onto the quieter path leading to the pavilion. 'You can rest assured that I won't inconvenience you tonight by leaving the pavilion. I promise I'll stay there all night. And now, as it's such a short walk from here—'

'I will come with you.'

Shazim had stepped in front of her. A few remaining villagers turned to look. She did the only thing she could. She bid them goodnight with a smile, and allowed their Sheikh to lead her on. She would deal with Shazim when they reached the pavilion and were alone.

CHAPTER ELEVEN

SHE WAS TENSE, but needn't have worried. Her overactive imagination was destined to be confounded at every twist and turn. Far from following her into the pavilion, and seducing her at great length and pleasure on the silken cushions, Shazim left her at the entrance with the sketch of a mocking bow, as if he knew exactly what she was thinking, and her naivety amused him.

Which only made her feel more frustrated than ever, fool that she was! Why was she having so much difficulty controlling her fantasies? Since the assault she'd not been able to think about such things, as the thought made her stomach knot, so the effect Shazim was having on her was altogether confusing!

Allowing the tent flap to fall back, she closed her eyes in disappointment. Any thoughts of fending him off resided solely in her mind, where they had to stay. And what a joke, when Shazim wasn't even interested.

And an affair with him would be crazy.

Yes. It would be crazy.

She began to pace. She wasn't even sure what she wanted, but it wasn't this after the excitement of the evening. She wasn't ready to go to sleep yet. She'd seen so much, experienced so much, and now she wanted more. Even this grand and special space was meant for sharing. There was so much here to enjoy and appreciate. Patterned carpets in jewel colours covered the floor, while the walls boasted hangings, embroidered with the royal emblems, as well as many other symbols she presumed were associated with Shazim. The silken cushions did indeed gleam beneath a honeyed light, just as she had always imagined, while the regal bed had been prepared for the night, and looked more than inviting— this huge, beautifully dressed bed, in which she would sleep alone.

Peeling off the diaphanous robe, she draped it carefully over an intricately carved ebony chair. Slipping on the simple nightshirt she'd brought with her 'just in case', she climbed into bed and tried to settle. The sheets held the scent of sunshine and sandalwood...

Like the man who ruled here—

With a frustrated growl, she thumped the pillows in an attempt to bounce Shazim out of her head. Making herself comfortable again, she turned her face into the cushions. She wouldn't think about him. She had no intention of compromising her professional standing in Shazim's eyes by doing anything she might regret.

Which wasn't enough to stop her body from longing for things it couldn't have.

Like Shazim, she mused groggily as she drifted off to sleep.

She was in the middle of a frenzied erotic episode, starring a shadowy figure clad in flowing robes, when she was rudely jolted awake. Catapulting off the bed, it took her a moment to realise that what she was listening to was the howling of a furious gale. This was the ear-splitting roar of nature at her most destructive. The sandstorm Shazim had talked about had arrived. When she'd read about storms like this on the Internet, they had made Shazim's homeland seem even more exciting and challenging, but to be in the middle of one, and to know that there was only camel skin and tent poles between her and the deadly wind, was a terrifying thought. The walls of the pavilion weren't billowing, as per her fantasy; they were straining to the limit of their resistance. It was as if some giant hand were trying to pluck the massive tent out of the ground. For a moment she was struck by panic, but then she remembered the animals.

Tugging on her clothes, she wrapped Shazim's

scarf around her face and neck. Then, raising her arm to protect her eyes, she forced her way out of the pavilion. She had to battle a wind so strong she could only lurch crazily from one solid structure to the next, grabbing hold of whatever came within reach to keep her balance.

Propelling herself forward took all her strength. Her goal was the clinic, and nothing was going to stop her from getting there. If she was frightened, the animals would be terrified. Some of them might even have been injured when they were thrown into a panic.

The clinic was only a short walk away under normal conditions, but with the lack of visibility, and the power of the wind, it seemed to take for ever to get there. It was only when she reached for the door handle, she realised, that any uncovered skin had been all but flayed by the driving sand. She was relieved to find the rangers in attendance, a little less so to see Shazim standing in their midst, staring at her with disapproval.

'What are you doing here?' he barked.

'My job,' she fired back.

'You need to dress those wounds,' he said in a tone that suggested she had caused more trouble than they needed by braving the storm.

'I'll do that later,' she said briskly. 'I'll wear gloves for now.' She was already pulling them on. 'You'll have to get out of my way,' she added, assuming command of the emergency clinic. 'Can you handle the bigger animals outside?' she asked Shazim, ignoring his look of surprise. 'If I have to, I'll do it, but it will stop me from working here,' she said impatiently in answer to his enraged expression.

'You should not have risked your life to join us,' he said coldly. 'We need you alive and uninjured. I thought I'd made that clear?'

He was right, but she was here, and she was staying here to work. 'Let's get on,' she said, staring up unblinking.

'Very well,' he conceded grimly. 'If you're staying I'll work alongside you.'

'As my assistant?' she challenged.

'As anything you need me to be. We have the same goal.'

'Then, if you will please triage the animals outside, and bring them to me one by one in order of need.'

'I will,' Shazim confirmed, summoning the rangers.

Isla lost all sense of time as she worked. The number of animals needing treatment never seemed to diminish. She rushed outside at one point to check on progress, only to find Shazim working harder than ten men in the paddock where the injured animals were being shepherded into covered stalls. It was quite a bit later before he joined her in the clinic, by which time he was grey with dust, and his eyes were as ringed and sore as hers.

She couldn't have been more surprised when he crossed the room and took her face in hands turned gentle.

'Must you always be such a hero, Isla?'

'This is what I came for. I'm in for everything, not just the celebrations.'

Shazim stared at her. 'You have many scratches. Let me clean them and dress them. You must be exhausted,' he added as he reached for the antiseptic.

'And you're not?' she said.

When Shazim looked at her there were things she didn't want to think about too closely, and the least of those was exhaustion. Their faces were so close as he cleaned her scratches their breath mingled, and when she glanced into his eyes she had to look away. She was in serious danger of getting carried away again. As the seconds ticked by, her entire body seemed to call to his in a way it had never done before.

'Let me clean you up now,' she insisted briskly when Shazim had finished tending her wounds.

'I heal fast.' He pulled away. 'Come with me, Isla. You've done enough tonight. I'll take you back to the pavilion.'

'I won't leave until I'm sure that every animal is calm and settled. I'm sorry, Shazim,' she added with an apologetic shrug when his eyes flared with disapproval at yet another example of her stubborn refusal to do as he commanded. 'I can't automatically obey, unless it makes sense to do so,' she explained. 'Obedience isn't in my job description, you see.' She smiled, and was relieved when Shazim laughed too.

'You are impossible,' he admitted with a shake of his head.

'You'll get used to me.'

'Will I?' He raised a brow.

Suddenly, she was on the back foot again, wondering if she would be in Q'Aqabi long enough for Shazim to 'get used to her'.

She started to protest when he called for one of the rangers to take her place.

'They managed very well without you,' he said firmly, 'and I expect them to do the same when you're not here.'

Straightening up with a hand in the small of her back, she closed her eyes for a moment to try and rattle some sense into her brain, but she was too tired to think.

'Isla?' Shazim demanded with concern.

Their determined stares met and held. She had to admit she was exhausted—and grateful to Shazim for working so tirelessly at her side. She wasn't going to argue with him for the sake of it.

'Bed,' he insisted, 'or you'll be no use to anyone tomorrow. If I have to throw you over my shoulder and carry you out of here, you're done for the night.'

It surprised her to see the air outside tinged with dawn. The wind had dropped and, though the air was still thick with dust, the visibility had improved. There was no immediate danger to the animals—

'That was a direct order,' Shazim insisted, cutting through her thoughts. 'You rest, or you go back to the city. Your choice, Isla. I won't have anyone working on this project who isn't as committed to safety as they are to doing their job.'

'The building site all over again,' she murmured, smiling faintly.

'The desert is a lot more dangerous than that.'

She had no doubt as Shazim stared at her, and another pulse of awareness joined the rest. Where was he going to sleep? She doubted he'd had time to make those *other* arrangements. She had read somewhere that Shazim was destined to marry in the near future so he could found a dynasty. She guessed he would choose a royal princess, or an heiress who understood the responsibilities that went with extreme wealth and privilege. If she were foolish enough to follow her heart, she might as well lay it on the ground for Shazim to stamp on.

'Bed,' Shazim instructed in a louder voice.

'Fine, fine. Do you trust me to find my way back this time?' She set her fingers flying to box up the remaining liniment and bandages, so she didn't have to look at the answer on Shazim's face.

'I probably should trust you to get back on your own,' he agreed, surprising her.

She glanced up, and knew at once that her disappointed look had betrayed her.

'Thank you for your assistance tonight,' she said primly, in a vain hope that she could deflect the calculating expression in Shazim's eyes.

'It was my pleasure to work with you,' he said. She breathed a sigh of relief at his acceptance of the change of subject. 'You seem to have settled in.'

'Oh, I have,' she enthused. 'It's so wonderful here.'

'Even the sandstorm?' he demanded drily.

'Apart from that,' she conceded. And then she felt prompted to ask, 'Did you find somewhere to stay tonight?'

Shazim had closed his eyes, and now he opened one of them. 'Why? Are you offering?'

'Certainly not,' she retorted. 'But you must be as tired,' she added, feeling guilty.

He raised a brow. 'Are you questioning my stamina?'

Shazim moved so fast, she was in no way ready for it, and she was pinned against the wall before she knew what was happening, with Shazim's fists planted on either side of her face. For a tense few seconds as he caged her, she was certain he was going to kiss her. 'What?' she challenged.

'I'm going to clear something up,' he said. His dark, mocking gaze dropped to her lips. 'You asked where I'm going to sleep tonight. Where do you think I'm going to sleep?'

'I have no idea. Maybe you've got a bed roll?' she guessed, as her heart did its best to beat its way out of her chest.

Was she really going to let him sleep outside in all that dust and fug? Wasn't she bigger than that?

'You're coming back with me to the pavilion,' she said bluntly. 'We both need to get some sleep.'

At least he had the good grace to look surprised by her offer.

'And, if you did have it in mind to seduce me—which I'm quite sure you don't—you'd better know that you'd have to wake me up first.'

'Is that so?' Shazim curved a smile as he pulled his fists away from the wall. 'You're taking a lot for granted, aren't you?'

'Seriously, Shazim—' She put on her most serious work face. 'Come back with me. At least try to get a few hours' sleep. There's plenty of food and drink, and you can bathe in the oasis.'

'Thank you for telling me that.' His smile reminded her who was the expert here. 'I can't think of anything I need more right now than a swim in ice cold water.'

CHAPTER TWELVE

'I CAN'T BELIEVE you're doing this for me,' Shazim murmured in his usual mocking tone as they reached the entrance of the pavilion.

'Shazim, I'd do this for an animal.'

His laugh was so free, so uninhibited, that she began to doubt her decision to allow him to stay. Shazim didn't sound in the least bit tired.

'I'll accept your kind offer, on one condition,' he said, drawing her attention to his shadowed face.

Alarm bells immediately started ringing. 'Yes? What's that?'

'You allow me to check your wounds before you go to bed.'

That seemed reasonable. She could hardly refuse.

'You were so impatient at the clinic, I'm not happy that I dealt with half of them as thoroughly as I would have liked…' As Shazim held the tent flap back and she walked past him into the pavilion, she felt like a piece in a game of chess that had just been held in check.

Bathing wounds should not be this pleasurable, she thoughts minutes later, frowning as Shazim's touch became seductive, rather than strictly therapeutic. 'Haven't you attended to that scratch before?'

'I didn't have this cream at the clinic,' he explained. 'We have special herbal remedies in Q'Aqabi—for just about everything,' he added with a smile, 'and there just happened to be some here.'

She watched as he dipped his big hand into a golden casket containing the healing potion. It was hard to believe he could be so gentle, or that she could remain obedient and still for quite so long.

'You're smiling?' he queried.

And she wasn't about to share the thought. She had sustained quite a few minor injuries during her training, but doubted that any of those big animals had been half as dangerous as Shazim.

'Better?' he murmured. Satisfied with his handiwork, he sat back, but as she went to tentatively touch her face he caught hold of her hand and kept it firmly in his grasp. 'No touching,' he whispered. 'Only I am allowed to do that.'

'Okay,' she agreed with a shrug. As long as it was only her face he was thinking of touching.

'You seem nervous, Isla.'

'Do I?' Was it so obvious? Intimacy between a man and a woman was so far out of her comfort zone she was surprised she hadn't jumped off the bed by now, but she had seen tenderness in Shazim's eyes, and it was hard to be frightened of that.

Was she falling for him?

Certainly not, Isla told herself impatiently. She would never lose sight of the fact that Shazim was the leader of a country, or that she was a vet on a mission to that country.

'We should call a halt to this,' she suggested, 'or I'm going to fall asleep.'

'No, you're not,' Shazim assured her.

Time seemed to stand still. His hands were so soft on her face, and as they moved down to her shoulders, and on her neck, and then her breasts, she didn't find them threatening at all. Shazim mapped her body so skilfully, so confidently, that she could only receive his touch and wonder why she had put this moment off for so long.

'You're not just a vet, Isla, you're a very beautiful woman.'

Easing her neck, she closed her eyes, wanting to believe him. Shazim's touch was like heady wine. He made her feel beautiful, when she feared that wasn't the case. He made her feel womanly, when she'd always striven to be practical and resolute. He made her make time for indulging in sensation and pleasure, which was something she had never done. His hands and touch were so knowing and instinctive that he made her body ache for him, but he knew just when to pull back.

'More?'

The question was in his eyes, and this time she could find no argument.

Weighing her breasts appreciatively, Shazim smiled deeply into her eyes. 'You were made for pleasure as well as practicality,' he insisted with a smile. 'Never forget that, Isla.'

She was never likely to while Shazim's thumbnails were lightly abrading her nipples. She closed her eyes and realised then that she had never known sensation like it. When she opened her eyes again, she decided she had never seen Shazim's eyes so mesmeric before, and realised then that he liked to watch the waves of pleasure building inside her. She'd had no idea that pleasure was such a skill, or that it could be so addictive. He was backing her down on the bed and she wasn't even resisting. Far from trying to find that practical part of her that always saved the day, she wanted it to be lost for ever. There was a very small part of her that questioned her sanity in inviting him to stay the night, but it couldn't compete with the pleasure waves consuming her.

And then he moved and stood up, and reality came flooding back in.

'You'll sleep on the floor?' she asked anxiously, not knowing why he'd suddenly broken away from her. Even to her, her voice seemed to have risen an octave.

He just stood there, looking deeply into her eyes; she felt thoroughly examined…and she liked it.

Slipping off the bed, she reached for the cushions and tossed them on the floor. 'There's no point in being uncomfortable,' she said. 'The floor rugs are thick, and with these cushions to lie on—'

Shazim caught her up in his arms. 'Stop,' he murmured. Nuzzling her neck with his sharp black stubble, he whispered, 'You don't have to hide behind cushions and rugs and excuses, Isla. Free yourself, and stop this now—'

'But I can't—I…I won't!' With a supreme effort, she managed to pull away from him, and, turning her back, she hugged herself tensely.

'Take the bed,' Shazim commanded softly, clearly defeated. 'You're exhausted. We'll talk about this some other time.'

She was so relieved that Shazim had no intention of taking advantage of the situation that she wanted to cry. Her emotions were in shreds, and she was too tired to think anything as she crawled into bed. She barely had the strength to strip down to her top and thong before crumpling on the pillows in an exhausted heap. Pretty much everything after that was a blur. She couldn't even remember pulling the covers up. It was so quiet after the noise of the storm that she slept like a baby. It was only when some goat bells woke her later that morning that she realised she had slept like a baby *in Shazim's arms*.

Catapulting off the bed, she staggered backwards until the walls of the tent prevented her from going any further. She frowned as she tried to work it out. At what point during the night had Shazim joined her on the bed?

Calming herself, she absorbed the facts. She was still dressed in her top and thong, while Shazim was sprawled...*naked* on the bed. His bronzed skin bore no traces of the sandstorm. He was clean and gleaming, his thick black hair glossy again.

He'd been for a swim, and though she knew she should look away, he was built like a titan, and it was hard—no, impossible—to do the right thing. She couldn't even control her breathing, which was coming hard and fast. She crept closer, taking advantage of his unconscious state. Shazim was as magnificent asleep as he was commanding when he was awake. She was glad he was sleeping on his front, though even his back view was a breath-stealing delight. Now she wondered how they'd both fitted on the bed. With his limbs sprawled, Shazim took up most of it...

That was why she had been curled into a tiny ball.

Yes. But a tiny ball in his arms!

'Are you coming back to bed?' Shazim murmured with his face still turned into the pillows. 'Or, are you going to stand there thinking about it for the rest of the day?'

Was he talking in his sleep? He had to be, surely?

She stared at his back, at the width of his shoulders, and at the tightness of his buttocks, and his hard-muscled thighs, all perfectly displayed for her pleasure. He was quiet again now, breathing easily, his entire glorious, bronzed body hers to admire.

The only excuse she could think of, as she remained perfectly still at the side of the bed, for how she'd ended up in his arms, was that when Shazim had returned from his swim he must have collapsed exhausted on the bed. He had probably taken hold of her while he was sleeping, perhaps mistaking her for someone else—

Her heart lurched and sank as she thought about it.

And what he'd said just now?

He'd said in his sleep, she reasoned. *Face facts.*

Shazim could have any woman he wanted. She had probably been having one of her heated dreams, sighing and moaning, so that taking hold of her was nothing more than a reflex action on his part. She could only hope she hadn't been talking in her sleep. Panic struck her now, at the thought of what she might have said—done—to encourage Shazim to mistake her for that someone else. She had to be grateful that the goat bells had woken her, Isla concluded.

So what now? She could hardly get back into bed. She was tempted to go for a swim. It would be the fastest way for her to wake up and clean the sand and grit off her body—and maybe the icy water would knock some sense into her head. With a rushed explanation to Shazim, who might be sleeping, that she was going for a swim, she made her escape outside.

She walked down to the banks of the oasis. There was no one to be seen, but she didn't need to strip off completely, as a thong and lightweight cotton top were fine for swimming. One last glance around, and she let herself down gently, gasping at the change in temperature. She had no fear of swimming alone. She was a strong swimmer, and she would take it steadily as she aimed for the opposite bank. Dipping her head beneath the water, she streamlined her body, and, using a strong, even stroke, she set off. A swim would ease her aching muscles, if nothing else.

It didn't seem to be helping anything else, like cooling her senses, she accepted as her thoughts flew back to the mystery of her night with Shazim.

He hadn't touched her.

She huffed a laugh at that—*As if!*—almost choking herself in the process.

No. Shazim hadn't touched her, and, truthfully, she wasn't sure whether to be insulted or relieved.

Relieved! Of course she was relieved. If he'd made a move she would have run a mile. She had experienced the usual teenage fumbling, but that one terrifying episode at her mother's funeral had finished her where sex was concerned. The man, who had assured her he was a good friend of her mother's, had tried to rape her, and had almost succeeded. She had fought him off, but it was a horror she would never forget.

The abuse he'd heaped on her afterwards had stayed with her ever since: she was unattractive and useless, anyway. No man would ever want her. He'd only been doing her a favour. After losing her mother, she had been at her lowest ebb, and the man's comments had left her devastated and defeated. The only type of sex she had indulged in since was in her head, where she was always in control. Shazim didn't need to know this. He would never know.

She raised her head mid-stroke to look around to check she was still alone. She had swum further away from the pavilion than she had intended, and it was time to go back and think about work. Stepping out of the water, she yielded to one last temptation. Closing her eyes, she turned her face to the sun and, stretching out her arms, she allowed the strengthening rays to dry her.

He watched Isla swimming and admired her strength—in the water and out of it. She was still battling her demons as he was, he suspected, though right now, standing in supplication to the sun on the bank, she looked as free as he'd ever seen her. He didn't want to change that, because it told him that Isla would reach her goal. At one time he might have seen her as a tender green shoot, but on closer acquaintance...she'd been a revelation to him during the storm. Brave and quick thinking, Isla had been as appealing to him in work mode as she had been at the celebration in the village, when she'd had all the appearance of an ethereal butterfly. Once again, she had proved to be so much more than that. At the campfire, she had achieved with smiles and gestures a connection with his people that had won her many friends. During the storm her bravery and resilience had won her the respect of his rangers. And in the early hours of this morning, stretched out on his bed, she had tempted him beyond reason.

And now?

For the next couple of days he would have her to himself. There was no hurry. Delay was arousing.

'Shazim!'

'I'm sorry if I startled you.'

'You didn't,' Isla insisted as she wrapped her arms around her chest. Her top was wet and plastered to her breasts. She'd had the presence of mind to remove her bra before falling asleep last night.

'Last night,' she began, as if picking up on at least some of his thoughts.

'You're not needed this morning,' he cut in.

'Not needed?' She frowned. 'Did I do something wrong?'

'On the contrary. The rangers agree with me that you should take a rest today after working through the night.'

'But that's not what I'm here for,' she argued. 'If there's a problem, we stand together.'

'There is no problem today, and the rangers are content to stand alone.'

The rangers were hardly going to disagree with their Sheikh, she thought.

'Don't worry, you'll be working,' Shazim assured her, seeing her doubt. 'I'm going to take you deeper into the desert, to a watering hole where you can witness the progress of the conservation programme first hand.'

'Will we stay overnight?'

'Is that your first question?'

'There are more.'

'Well, to answer the first one, the length of our stay will depend on what we find when we get there.'

'I'll be prepared,' she said.

'I'm counting on it.' He wisely curbed a smile.

If this was work she couldn't refuse, Isla reasoned as she walked swiftly back to the pavilion to prepare to leave, her main concern was this: Was Shazim trialling her for a job he had in mind, or something else? And what could she do about it, either way?

CHAPTER THIRTEEN

ISLA STAYING ON in Q'Aqabi was now a definite in his mind, rather than a possibility, but how would she feel when he took a bride? *How would he feel?* The villagers might have taken to Isla on sight, but the country was agitating for him to get married. When he did that, his bride would be chosen from a similar background, and would understand that any marriage he contracted would be a transaction to the benefit of both parties. He wasn't free to indulge in the idea of romance. It simply didn't exist in his world. His duty was to his country, and to his late brother, and that called for nothing less than single-minded dedication to the cause.

'I really need to stay here at the clinic quite a lot longer,' Isla said, frowning.

'You're having doubts now?' he queried sharply. 'I thought you were looking forward to visiting the interior with me?'

She hummed uncertainly. 'I'm only just beginning to realise the scope of the job here, and I need time to establish myself at the clinic.'

His male pride was piqued. Isla's eyes were wary and she couldn't hold his stare, suggesting there was a lot more than the clinic on her mind. His best guess was she didn't trust herself to go deeper into the wilderness with him.

'The clinic isn't going anywhere. It will still be here when you get back.'

Her jaw firmed as if she had come to a decision. His mind was made up, and he was impatient now, both to leave, and to have Isla with him. His hunger for her was growing like a sharp, nagging edge. She would come with him. There was no more to be said on the matter.

Shazim had made it impossible for her to refuse to take the trip, but she was going to make a few of her own rules before they set off. For a start, she was going to ride her own horse. She wouldn't risk any more of that pressing up close against him. This was a research trip, not a romantic outing.

Riding her own horse was perhaps an exaggeration. The animal the rangers brought up for her was more of a plodding mule. But it was kind, and its ears were velvety beneath her fingertips. It was just an old horse, slow and steady. They'd get on fine, she told herself confidently, as Shazim rode up on his fire-breathing monster.

'I see you've already mounted up,' he said with the suggestion of an amused smile.

'And *I* see that you are resigned to riding alone without my assistance,' she countered as she gathered up the reins.

'Like this,' he said, leaning over.

He was just gorgeous, and his hands on hers were a seductive delight, but she pretended not to notice as Shazim laced the reins through her fingers.

He was a great guide too, and took trouble to point out all the things she wouldn't have noticed without him as they rode along: ibexes concealed in the shadow of a dune, and animal tracks, and then, most thrillingly, a pair of desert eagles soaring high above their heads. But it was when they rounded the base of a particularly mountainous dune that she got the biggest surprise of all.

'My observation post,' Shazim explained with the flash of a grin and a casual shrug.

She couldn't tell if he was joking or not, for there, sitting on the bank of the most beautiful and tranquil watering hole, was the billowing Bedouin tent of her fantasies.

'Is this what you pictured when you set out for Q'Aqabi?' he demanded, turning in the saddle to take a look at her.

'Pretty much,' she admitted, feeling her cheeks fire red.

'My people will have set up refreshments for us, but I suggest a swim first to cool off.'

'Sounds good,' she agreed. What was she worried about? Shazim hadn't even mentioned sleeping with her last night. He'd been all business since they left the village.

Didn't that make her feel just the tiniest bit disappointed?

No. It did not. This trip was to inform her about the project and nothing more. Shazim's people had been out here ahead of them to set up the equipment they would require for...well, for whatever they were here for.

She soon forgot her concerns when Shazim led the way into the icy water. Her much smaller mount followed his, and soon they were swimming, their horses lunging forward. She was getting the hang of this—

Or, she thought she was, until the force of the water lifted her clean out of the saddle.

Shazim's hand instantly found her thigh and he pushed her deep into the rolling motion of the saddle. She gasped as her body accepted the contact—of him, and of the horse's thrusting gait. Sensations collided: the cold of the water and the heat of his hand, and he didn't take his hand away, leaving his fingertips within millimetres of her core.

'Better now?' he asked.

Was that amusement in his voice? Rather than answer him, she decided to concentrate on staying on the horse.

'That was great,' she admitted as their horses found solid ground and clambered out. The magic of the desert must be getting to her, she concluded.

Once they were safely on dry land, she dismounted cautiously, determined not to make the same mistake again. She was becoming more confident on a horse. She would need to be, to get about in the desert. Taking the reins over her horse's head, she tethered him where Shazim had left his stallion.

'Isla…' She turned at Shazim's call. And then had to try to appear as if seeing the most beautiful man stark naked was all in a day's work for her.

What had she expected—that he would pull out a pair of designer swimming shorts from his saddlebag?

This was the desert. Life was in the raw. She had known what to expect when she came out here. Didn't she pride herself on being practical and down to earth?

Yes. But she hadn't expected to be confronted by the sight of Shazim diving butt naked into the watering hole.

'Do I have to come there and get you?' he shouted to her from the water.

Please no!

But. There was only one way to handle this. Planting her hands on her hips, she gave him a look, and then, slowly and deliberately, she peeled off her clothes.

He had turned away by this time, but he heard Isla entering the water. He badly needed an outlet for his energy, and had powered away to the opposite bank. He turned to see Isla swimming strongly towards him.

She remained a safe distance away, treading water. 'Race?' she suggested, her face innocent and beautiful.

'I'll give you a head start,' he offered.

'Do you really think I need one?' she queried, lifting a brow.

'I know you do.'

It was only when she turned away and started swimming that he realised she was as naked as he was. And there had been a definite blaze of challenge in her eyes. Now he knew why. With a laugh he powered after her. Isla Sinclair was determined to beat him at his own game. It remained to be seen if she could.

He followed at a lazy pace, knowing how badly she wanted to win. She still felt she had something to prove to him, but she was wrong. Isla had nothing to prove to him.

She stopped swimming in the shallows, trying to decide what to do next. Maybe she wasn't as brazen as she thought she was.

When he reached her, she whipped her arm across the surface of the water, sending a blinding spray into his face.

'Two can play at that game, Ms Sinclair—'

'I certainly hope so,' she yelled back at him.

She was frightened by what she'd started with Shazim; excited and aroused. There was no mistaking her feelings now. Whatever fear there had been had been replaced by a far more primal need, and it was inevitable that what had started out as fun turned serious. They tangled in the water, and Shazim wrapped his arms around her. She could feel every impressive inch of him against her. There was a moment when they stilled and looked at each other...

Isla's eyes had darkened in a way he couldn't mistake. He had an instant to decide if he needed this sort of complication in his life.

'Who knew?' she said, pushing him away. 'You can be fun.'

'You have no idea,' he murmured.

Letting her go, he lifted his hands, palms up flat, to signal once and for all that this was over. But then she did the last thing he'd been expecting. Still laughing, she threw herself back into his arms, and, lunging forward, she planted a clumsy kiss on his lips.

'Don't,' he warned, slowly wiping the back of his hand across his mouth. 'You don't know what you're getting yourself into.'

'Maybe I do,' she argued stubbornly, holding his gaze as they stood facing each other in the shallows.

They looked at each other, daggers drawn for a moment, and then he swung her into his arms and strode with her to the tent.

Shazim didn't speak. He didn't need to. She knew what she was doing. Even knowing what she had here and now with Shazim was only temporary, she had made the first move, and she was quite prepared to see it through.

What exactly did she have with Shazim?

If anyone was going to help her to shake her fear of sex—

She had fallen for him.

Maybe.

Definitely. Was she prepared to pay such a heavy price for what could only be a few hours of pleasure?

She had never been a coward.

She'd never been a fool, either.

Her inner critic's plain talk was wasted. All she

wanted was Shazim. For however long it lasted, everything had been leading up to this moment. The desert had awoken something primal in her, and that had freed her as he'd said it would.

Once they were inside the pavilion, Shazim took her face in his hands in a touch so gentle it was almost reverent. He made her feel safe, valued. But then something changed in his gaze that made a prescient shiver trickle down her spine. He was probably thinking the same thing she was: that this was just a moment in time, and that it couldn't last. But while it did…

Linking their fingers, he very slowly drew her close. She breathed deep on his familiar scent with its overtones of sandalwood. She loved his touch. She loved being this close to him. She loved the way her skin tingled with awareness.

When Shazim brushed his mouth against hers, she softened against him. When he deepened the kiss, she clung hungrily to him. He might be a king, and powerful beyond imagining, but in this they were equals.

'I'm glad that fate has brought you here,' he said, removing the last of her doubts.

Pressing her body against his, she was suddenly ravenous for more contact, the ultimate contact. This was her man, her mate. As their tongues tangled and her breathing quickened, her fate was sealed. Shazim was air for her lungs, and food for her soul, and his kisses were a seduction she couldn't resist. Her body ached for him to be deep inside her. He was the missing part of her, and the cure for her deep-seated fears. She answered Shazim's fierce passion with hungry sounds of need, until with a growl he let her go. And when she sank down on the bed, he hooked his thumb into the back of his robe and dragged it over his head. Her eyes widened as she stared at him, naked and magnificent, like a statue cast in bronze. Tossing the robe aside, he threw the covers back and joined her on the bed. He was such a daunting sight. He was so huge, so beautiful—

And was entirely built to scale—

Those old memories made her want to run away…this was too much…

'Isla?'

Crouched on all fours, she was starting to back her way off the bed. Shazim drew her back to him. 'No,' he said. 'That's not the way. You don't run from anything, Isla, least of all me.' And while she was still hesitating, and still unsure, he embraced her again, bringing her close so he could soothe her with unthreatening kisses until she calmed down.

He had been right all along about Isla, but she was far more damaged than he knew. He held her for a long time until her eyes started to close, and then he settled her back on the pillows and stood up.

'No,' she exclaimed groggily, her confidence returning. As he threw on his robe she reached for his hand. 'You're right. I don't run from anything.'

He backed away. This was torture for him, but it was torture he would gladly bear for her sake. He might want Isla with a madness that threatened his usual control, but her need was far greater than his, and he would not take advantage of her fears. She was clearly not ready for this. Not ready for him. She was inviolable until she was strong enough to share the cause of them.

'I'm not leaving you,' he explained, 'but you must tell me who has hurt you. If you don't let the poison out, it will destroy you.'

It was a relief when she began haltingly to explain. He sat in a chair to listen a little way from the bed. He didn't want to do or say anything to interrupt her. He needn't have worried. It was as if she had lanced a wound, and all the foulness of the past poured out. It appeared that, on top of the tragedy of losing her mother, Isla had been further traumatised. He listened to her story in horror, and when she'd finished he went back to the bed and took her into his arms. 'Not all men are like that, Isla. Give life a chance. Learn to trust again, or this will scar you for ever.'

While Isla knew, deep in her heart, that his words spoke the truth, something defensive rose up in her.

'Says the Sheikh with shadows in his eyes,' she murmured.

His whole expression changed in a moment. She saw the hurt and pain in his eyes and instantly regretted her words.

Standing, he turned away. Dressing again, he slipped his feet into his sandals and left the tent.

She didn't call him back this time.

CHAPTER FOURTEEN

ISLA BRINGING UP the past had really thrown him, but work had always been his salvation. Thankfully, there was no shortage of work to do. They were still at the watering hole, where he was separating the pregnant ibexes from the rest of the herd, when Isla joined him. She acted as if nothing unusual had happened between them. That suited him. They'd get more done.

They worked side by side until the sun went down, and they worked on by moonlight. When the moon finally went behind a cloud, he called it a day.

'That's it. We'll start again tomorrow.'

They walked back together to the tent, but he stopped when he reached the supplies he'd decanted from his saddlebags.

'What are you doing?' Isla asked him.

'Preparing to sleep beneath the stars…'

'There's no need for that,' she said awkwardly as he rolled out his sleeping mat.

'I could sleep on the floor of the tent,' he suggested tongue in cheek, 'but I prefer to sleep out here.'

'Then, so do I,' she blurted out.

'You?' He stared at her in astonishment. Even though she'd opened her heart to him, after her last brush with intimacy he had imagined Isla would want to forget being close to him. 'No.' He shook his head. 'You sleep under cover. You're not used to sleeping rough.'

'You'd be surprised what I'm used to—'

He cursed beneath his breath as she disappeared inside the tent, and then stared at the sky and asked for patience when she returned loaded down with blankets and cushions.

'Let me,' she said, dumping them on the ground so she could dip down to help him clear some rocks away. 'I'm sorry,' she whispered, glancing up.

'What are you sorry for?'

'For loading my troubles onto you—can we start again?'

She took his silence for refusal. 'Please?'

She came right up to him, and looked so young and sexy. 'Better not,' he said.

'But our working relationship's still okay?'

Her tone was anxious. 'Nothing's changed,' he assured her. Bed made, he stood up.

'Are you sure you're okay with that?' she asked, flashing a dubious glance at his bedroll.

'Why wouldn't I be?'

Taking hold of her shoulders, he brought her in front of him. The fire he'd made to combat the chill of a desert night crackled on, while the moon beamed down benevolently. Everything was as it should be, but he still got the feeling that everything in his rigidly controlled life was about to change.

'I think you'd rather be with me, in the tent,' she whispered.

'Have you learned nothing?' he demanded, putting her away from him. Impatiently, he toed the cushions into place.

As she reached for him it became clear that she had not. And this time he'd call her bluff.

Catching hold of her hand, he bit her palm gently, and when she gasped out loud he drew one of her fingertips into his mouth.

The air between them was electric as Shazim drew her deeper into his erotic net. Closing her eyes, she inhaled deeply and shakily as he dipped his head to lightly brush her lips with his. His kiss was like a question: Did she want to carry on? Her answer was yes, most certainly. This time she reached up and laced her fingers through his hair to keep him close. Her senses were full of him. He intoxicated her. He tasted of all things good. He smelled of woodsmoke and sandalwood, and the delicate balance between her fear of physical love and the growing sense that she was safe with him reached tipping point. Realistically, she was in the greatest danger of her life. Shazim's destiny called him to greater things than a girl by a campfire in the desert. But she had no intention of spending the rest of her life wondering what a night with Shazim would be like.

When his big hands cupped her buttocks, that delicate balance between safety and danger tipped irrevocably.

She groaned as he pressed her against him, and groaned again when she felt the thickness and weight of his erection. Her body seemed to mould around his of its own accord, and when he cupped her breasts over her fine cotton top she exhaled on a soft and shaking cry. She was glad, for once, that her breasts were so firm and big and full. She wanted him to like them. She was glad that her nipples were uptilted and tempting, and when he removed her top in one easy move and claimed the tight buds, laving first one and then the other with his tongue, she encouraged him to sink his face deep. Arching her back, she thrust her hips towards him to show how much she approved.

'Not yet,' Shazim murmured, slanting a wicked

smile as he glanced up at her. 'You must learn patience, *habibti*.'

She had no patience, no self-control, and writhed against him, seeking more contact.

'What do you need?' Shazim murmured, baiting her with his smouldering heat.

'I think you know,' she whispered.

'But you must tell me,' he insisted. 'Those are my rules.'

'*Your* rules?'

'Even now you are defiant?'

He frowned, but she could tell that the thought amused him.

'My rules, or nothing,' he said as he reached for the fastening on her shorts.

'Do you want to take a bet on that?' she said softly as she pushed his hand away. Slowly and deliberately, she lowered the zipper herself.

He loved Isla's defiance almost as much as her self-determination. She was ready, and it had been worth the wait. He wanted nothing to stand between them, least of all the past, or her unreasonable fear. He took over, sliding her shorts over the swell of her hips...slowly. He was in no rush. He intended to relish the sensation of his slightly roughened palms moving over her silky skin as he took her thong down.

He couldn't wait to tease and explore. He had

to remind himself, quite forcefully, that delay was always the servant of pleasure.

She gave a sharp intake of breath when he drew his robe over his head. That reaction was echoed by his own response as he stared down at her. The flames of the campfire had warmed Isla's pale skin to blush peach, while he remained in shadow and darkness. The contrast between them was marked and she was half his size.

'Shazim…' She reached for him. 'Touch me. Teach me—'

Pausing only to protect them both, he silenced her with a kiss. 'Not until you tell me what you want,' he reminded her.

'An end to this torture,' she said, but, as she was still covering herself modestly with her arms, she was doing nothing to convince him to speed things up.

'What torture?' he demanded, continuing to tease her with long strokes down the length of her thighs.

'My legs don't ache,' she said, frowning.

'You're getting used to riding,' he observed with the faintest of smiles.

He carried on stroking her as she sighed with pleasure, and then he moved his attentions to where she needed him, but he was never quite close enough.

'Shazim,' she begged him in a shaking voice.

'Good?' he murmured, teasing her some more.

'Not good enough,' she complained, and then she turned her face into the cushions, as if for once her boldness had gone too far, even for her.

Easing her legs over his shoulders, he made her lie back on the cushions while he knelt in front of her.

She was shocked, and exclaimed, 'What are you— Oh,' she gasped as he cupped her buttocks, holding her firmly in place. She was more aroused than even he had suspected.

Was it possible to survive sensation like this? Isla doubted it, and sucked in a shuddering breath as she clung to the bedroll at her side. Shazim was so good at this, so intuitive. He knew exactly when to draw back, and when to give her just a little bit more. Having dispensed with what remained of her modesty, he was keeping her legs widely spread on the powerful sweep of his shoulders. And she was right on the edge.

His tongue was slightly roughened and he knew just how much pressure to apply. The rhythm was irresistible, and she was just tensing to let go when he stopped.

She exclaimed with disappointment as he lowered her legs and sat back. But then he nudged one hard-muscled thigh between her legs, easing them apart again. She felt so exposed and so aware as he stared down, and she was so very desperate for contact, but all he would give her was the tip of his erection. Drawing it back and forth very lightly, he made her crave release. She hadn't even understood her own body when it came to her capacity to feel pleasure, but now she was hungry for more, and angled her body in an attempt to catch more of him.

'I need you,' she cried out in frustration.

'You need this,' he argued. 'Say it,' he commanded in a firmer tone.

'I need all of you,' she exclaimed, a slave to the hunger inside her. 'And I need it now,' she gasped, thrusting her hips up to meet him.

'I decide when,' Shazim murmured, taking the cry of disappointment from her mouth in a kiss. 'Slowly,' he warned when she fought hard to urge him on. 'I won't rush this, not even for you. I won't hurt you, Isla.'

And she believed him. Trusted him. Which was something she'd never thought she'd be able to do again. And then he touched her with his hand, and took her to yet another level of arousal.

'Tell me,' he whispered against her mouth. 'Tell me what you need.'

'I need you deep inside me,' she said shakily. 'I need you to take me deep. You're so big, I want you to let me get used to you first,' she pleaded on a suddenly dry throat, 'but then, I want you to take me firmly, fast and hard—'

Forced to break off, she wailed softly with excitement as Shazim caught inside her…and this time he didn't pull back. She remained quite still, savouring the moment, and then she exhaled on a gust of pleasure as he sank a little deeper still. He repeated this several times, sometimes withdrawing completely before returning to give her a little more each time. She trusted him completely, knowing now that if she tensed, he would stop. It was a lesson in how to relax, and her reward was Shazim's thick length deeply lodged inside her. When he rolled his hips she almost fell, but as always he knew how to keep her from the brink. He remained quite still, poised over her, braced on his forearms. He withdrew steadily until they were completely parted, and then, after a moment of fear that he might stop, he plunged deep. He moved hard and fast, driving into her with firm, regular strokes, shooting the air from her lungs and the fear from her heart, and with a cry of relief she threw herself into pleasure. When she quieted, he reduced the pace to a gentle and insistent buffeting, until she discovered that, far from her pleasure ending, it was just building again.

'Hold your legs wide for me,' Shazim instructed, staring down to where her enjoyment was all too obvious to him. 'And don't move. Your role is to lie still and be pleasured.'

His promise excited her, and she pressed her thighs apart.

'Relax,' he warned when she began to tense as her climax approached. 'If you don't relax, I'll stop. Now, concentrate your mind on that one place, and no other. Good,' he approved as she stilled.

Turning her onto her hands and knees, he moved behind her. His hands on her buttocks were firm and controlling as her hunger raged on. Anticipation of pleasure had made her insatiable, and when he took her and touched her, she couldn't hold on.

'Greedy,' he said approvingly as she rammed backwards onto him.

She worked her hips frantically to be sure of the last pulse of pleasure. Shazim barely gave her the chance to draw a breath this time before throwing her onto her back and taking her again, firmly and fast.

There was no world outside this, no existence possible outside the two of them, and there was no man for her ever, but Shazim.

He relished Isla's mewls of pleasure, and her final ecstatic cries. Even now she wasn't sated and reached for him. She was a revelation to him. Her appetite matched his. No sooner had she crested one wave than she eagerly sought out the next.

'But what about you?' she asked him finally.

'Me?' He laughed softly against her mouth as he dragged her close for a kiss. 'Don't you think I'm enjoying this?'

'I know you are,' she said, reaching down. He shuddered with pleasure as her small hand closed possessively around him.

'Then,' he instructed, 'you must mount me.'

'Must I?' She gave him a look. 'Do I need another riding lesson?'

'Oh, yes.'

'Then, I'm glad to obey, Your Majesty,' she said with a witchy smile. Rolling away, she changed position, and, arranging herself on top of him, she spread her legs wide. Throwing her head back, she groaned with pleasure as he guided her slowly down.

'You are a witch,' he remarked as she grew in confidence.

'And you're the best stallion I ever rode.'

She laughed, and he laughed with her as she attempted to pin him down.

Coming to Q'Aqabi, to do the job she loved, had altered Isla in one small, but fundamental way. She didn't just know what she wanted now, she knew how to get it. How he would ever let her go, he had no idea.

'Better?' he asked when she was calm enough to speak.

'Almost,' she teased him with a look. 'I feel there might be more.'

'Much more,' he confirmed, proving it.

'You're right,' she agreed with a gasp of pleasure.

Shazim made everything possible. She had never guessed she had such an exhaustive appetite. 'I love it,' she exclaimed in answer to his husky question.

I love you, she thought as Shazim turned her so her back was facing him.

'So I can touch you while I take you,' he explained.

'Whatever you want to do is all right by me.' She laughed softly, realising this was true. There was nothing Shazim could do that would frighten her, or that she wouldn't enjoy—though enjoy was hardly the word for it. There had to be a new word invented for this amount of pleasure. 'Oh, yes,' she breathed when he pressed the flat of his hand into the small of her back, making her even more available to him. 'It's so good… and I can't hold on—'

'You're not supposed to,' he reminded her, continuing to move to the same dependable rhythm. 'Just let go…'

He loved watching her face when Isla lost control, but watching from this angle gave him another view on pleasure. Keeping her buttocks firmly angled with one hand, he worked her sensitive bud with the other. At the same time he thrust rhythmically and deep. But Isla had some ideas of her own, and he groaned as she closed her inner muscles tightly around him.

'Let go,' she urged him, angling her buttocks even more for him to see. 'Let—'

The rest of her words were lost in a roar of mutual release as they fell together.

Pounding into her, he thought she might extract his life force before she'd finished with him. And when they did finally recover, they could do no more than collapse back on the bedroll and sleep.

Some time during the night he woke and watched her sleeping beside him. She looked so peaceful, so young and carefree, and so happy that he smiled in response to the curve of her lips as she slept. He wondered what she was dreaming about to make her smile. Then the fire started guttering, and a cool breeze reminded him that the temperature would dip further still. Gathering her into his arms, he carried her to the tent and laid her down on the bed, and this time he made no pretence of sleeping on the floor. Pulling her into his arms, he kissed her and drew the covers over both of them.

CHAPTER FIFTEEN

SHE WOKE SLOWLY, stretching out a body that had been very well used. She smiled as she remembered Shazim making love to her, and stretched out a lazy hand to touch him.

'Hey, lazy bones—'

She turned to see Shazim, already up and drying his wild black hair on a towel. There was another towel slung around his lean waist. He'd been for a swim, and his bronzed torso was pumped and gleaming. He looked amazing. Burying her face into the pillow, she faced up to the fact that she looked like the same sleep-wrecked, down-to-earth woman she'd always been, a woman who was far too sensible to ever be called pretty. In fact, forget pretty. A man like Shazim would hook up with a genuine beauty. It was one thing having a passionate fling with the ugly duckling, out in the desert with no one to see them, but he'd want the swan for when he was back in town.

'Come on,' he urged, leaning over her. 'It's time to get up and out.'

She pushed her worries aside. 'Kiss first,' she insisted, clinging onto the fantasy for as long as she could.

'We've got work to do,' he said sternly.

She loved his sternness. She loved the work. She loved the way he said, *we've* got work to do. The fact that Shazim was already thinking of them as a team, at least professionally, was all she had ever wanted. And they were a team—a great team.

At least for now.

Turning to face him, she smiled away her fears and reached up. 'This is something special, isn't it?' Now she sounded desperate, but she was too much in love to care.

He laughed. 'So special I may never get enough of you.'

Her heart actually ached with happiness. That was all she had wanted to hear.

He should have known it wouldn't end with a good morning kiss. The moment his hands closed around Isla's soft, hungry body, it was only a short trip to their favourite destination. Making her shriek with excitement as he swung her off the bed, he kissed her deeply as she wrapped her legs around him. Backing her up to one of the sturdy tent poles, he did the only decent thing.

'Oh, yes,' she exclaimed, working furiously to draw him inside her.

In a matter of moments they were working together and laughing softly against each other's mouths.

'One more time,' she begged him, writhing a little to encourage him.

He needed no encouragement and took her again.

These had been the best few days of her life, Isla thought, smiling as she helped Shazim to free some rare desert gazelles into the wild later that morning. They had shared something special. And the best thing about it—the part she couldn't believe—was that Shazim seemed to feel the same about her. He hadn't told her exactly that he loved her, but he had said that he could never get enough of her.

Okay, she was a realist, and Shazim was a king, a lord of the desert. They could never be a cosy couple, but they might work something out.

And when he gets married, as kings do?

She didn't know—she wasn't sure. That was a question for another day.

Forcing unwelcome thoughts out of her head, she got on with unlatching the crates to free the animals. Her heart swelled with love for Shazim as they exchanged a triumphant glance when the animals bounded free.

'And now I must go,' he said, shocking her into silence. 'I'll take a quick swim to freshen up, and then—'

'You're going already?' She had thought she was prepared for this. He'd said something about the rangers coming so she wouldn't be alone, but she'd been too busy working, and hadn't really listened. Shazim had explained that he had some matters of state to attend to, she remembered now, after which he would be meeting with some Q'Aqabian tribesmen. His departure was hardly a surprise. She just hadn't expected it to be so soon.

'An emergency,' he explained, frowning with concern. 'A dispute between some local tribesmen—if I'm not there to pass judgement it could blow up into something big.'

'Then, you must go,' she insisted. 'What?' she said when he hesitated.

'I don't want to leave you, Isla.'

'Don't be ridiculous. Of course you've got to go.' Pushing her hair back, she straightened up to confront him. 'Don't think I can't manage here.'

'The rangers are on their way to join you,' he murmured as if thinking out loud.

'There you are. Everything's fine. Now, go.'

'The last communication I had with the rangers said they'd be no longer than half an hour.'

'Then, what are you worrying about?'

He hummed in answer.

'Look,' she said, pointing out into the desert. 'You can see the dust from their Jeeps from here. They're even closer than you thought.'

'They'll have to leave the Jeeps with tribesmen, and travel on by horseback—'

'I know you wouldn't leave me if you thought there was the slightest danger.'

Only Shazim's eyes were visible now as he wound his *howlis* around his head. He was again the Lion of the Desert, and she knew exactly what she was taking on. They both had a job to do. 'Go,' she insisted. 'I wouldn't have agreed to come to Q'Aqabi in the first place if I hadn't thought I could handle situations like this.'

'There are plenty of supplies in the tent for all of you, so you can stay on and finish the job.' Shazim's stallion was becoming impatient as he added, 'The weather report is good, but remember that the desert is unpredictable.'

'I'll be fine,' she insisted, flinging her arms out wide. 'If I can't survive for twenty minutes on my own, what hope do I have of keeping a job here?'

Shazim still look worried as he made the customary gesture with his hand to his forehead, his lips, and then his heart, and she wondered if his concern had anything to do with those shadows in his eyes. He didn't give her time to ask him as he wheeled his horse and rode away.

Shazim was a king with duties to his country-men, Isla reasoned sensibly after watching him ride away until he had disappeared from sight. He could hardly take off endless amounts of time to be with her. She had always known that what they had would end abruptly, and maybe this was for the best. Shazim would come back, of that she had no doubt, but by then they would both have had chance to think, and to come to terms with a reality that did not include a long-term relationship between Shazim and his latest veterinary recruit.

The rangers did not arrive. Instead, Isla received a radio message to say that a flood warning had prevented them from taking the route they had intended, and that she must get herself to higher ground without delay. Shazim was already on his way back to her.

'If he's only coming to rescue me, he can stay where he is,' she insisted as her heart squeezed tight with concern for him.

'He's on his way, Ms Sinclair. There's nothing we can do to stop him now.'

She would have said more, but the radio signal crackled and then broke up.

Well, there was no sign of a flood so far, Isla reassured herself, and Shazim was as capable as she was of taking care of himself. But she still worried about him, and kept on checking the sky to be sure there was no sign of a storm. Maybe the flood warning was for somewhere else, she reasoned, somewhere closer to the rangers. If the worst happened, she had been watching the path the gazelles took up the cliff when they were released. They were wily animals and instinct invariably kept them safe. The pathways up the cliff were narrow, but manageable. She could only hope Shazim didn't take any chances with his safety. Dashing worried tears from her eyes, she got on with her work.

He could not believe what he'd done. He'd left Isla alone in the desert. Who knew better than he that conditions could change in minutes in the wilderness? In one final irony, as he'd ridden away he had told himself that he was doing the right thing, and that he should leave Isla for her own sake, to save her from him.

He'd made a critical error. If Isla was in danger, there was nowhere else he should be than at her side. He had issued a declaration to the tribesmen that if they didn't sort out their differences they would be answerable to him. Word from his council had come back immediately to say the

warring factions had parted grumbling, but resigned to obey their Sheikh's will.

Shazim was a strong ruler, and he should have
known better than to allow his feelings for Isla
to go so deep. He could not allow their relationship to progress, but that didn't mean he would
knowingly expose her to danger. He couldn't bear
to be responsible for another tragedy. And when
Isla was involved—

Leaning low over his stallion's neck, he urged
his horse to gallop even faster. He would reach
Isla—whatever it took.

He reined in abruptly. The outcrop of rock
where he'd left her was already awash with water.
The dried up riverbed was full. He'd have to go
around it. He tried to reach her by satellite phone,
but each time the line cut before she could answer; a sign that the weather conditions were de-
teriorating. He could only hope that she'd had the
good sense to move to higher ground. He scram-
bled helicopters from the royal fleet, but even he
couldn't be sure that they would arrive in time.

If he lost her—

Isla had more courage and can-do in her little
finger than anyone he'd ever met. He might be
wedded to his country, and to the projects that
had meant so much to his brother, but if this was
what caring for someone felt like, then he embraced it with all his heart, and the sooner he told

Isla how he felt about her, the sooner he might
be able to live with himself again. The realisa-
tion that she might be in danger had shaken him
to the core—it had unlocked something in him
and he knew, without a shadow of a doubt, that
he had to be with her, because he loved her. She
was his life.

There was no sign of Shazim, nor was there any
sign of an impending flood. There was an in-
crease in the flow of water in the riverbed, but
that was only consistent with a brief rainstorm
somewhere else. The sky was sullen overhead,
which was new in Isla's brief experience of the
desert, but there was nothing else to alarm her.
She had one more group of animals to tag before
the herd could be left to roam at will, and then
she would call it a day.

Or so she thought. But a few of the animals
were really wily, and had managed to escape. She
caught up with them further down the riverbed
on the flat ground that Shazim had warned her
to stay away from, as it could flood.

She would be quick, she reassured herself as
the deepening river water washed over her sand
boots.

She glanced up to where the rest of the herd
was waiting. Some of them were climbing higher
still. She stopped for a moment to listen, but

could hear nothing unusual. Maybe there was some tasty moss on the higher slopes.

It didn't take her long to finish and, as the last animals joined their companions, she shaded her eyes and smiled to see a group of horned faces staring down at her.

The last animal to be released was a fawn. It leapt up the jagged path like lightning, and Isla's stomach clenched when she saw its startled eyes and laid-back ears. She tried telling herself that no animal liked to be captured and tagged, and she had no reason to be fearful. She ducked instinctively as a crash of thunder argued with this. And then the rain came down. It didn't just start to fall, but hit her with the force of endless blows. She was drenched immediately.

So that was why the animals were so spooked. She'd done her homework, and she knew what could happen in a thunderstorm in the desert. After Shazim's warning, she took no chances and raced to the base of the cliff. Starting to scrabble up it, she knew she'd been overconfident and too absorbed in her work. She should have done this sooner. Her nails ripped on the treacherous surface as she struggled to find a handhold on the same path the gazelles had used. Desert sand didn't soak up water quickly, and the walls of water created by a sudden rainstorm could be as much as thirty feet high. She had to keep on climbing or she could drown. More people drowned in the desert than died of thirst, she had also read.

She reached a ledge and took a moment to catch her breath, but she still wasn't high enough. The animals were a long way above her, but they took chances, and she didn't have their blind courage. They would launch themselves into space on a wing on a prayer, but if they fell... She cried out as the fawn she'd just tagged spun past her. Jostled from the ledge by its companions, it had missed bouncing off the cliff face by only a hair's breadth. It landed awkwardly and she breathed a sigh of relief when, having righted itself, it shook its head. But it was dazed, and was bleating with bewilderment.

By this time she was halfway down the cliff on her way to rescue it. And now she could hear the water coming. Just the faintest rumble in the distance, but it was getting louder all the time.

He saw the flash flood coming while he was safe on higher ground. The only way he could be sure that Isla wasn't trapped was to climb the cliff where they'd been working from the other side.

When he reached the top and looked over the edge, the sheer volume and force of the water was far worse than he'd imagined. He had supplies in his saddlebag, including rope, gloves, and a medical kit, all of which was a necessary precaution in the wilderness. And he knew how to climb. He also knew just how dangerous it could be. In fact, who knew better than he, when his climbing had been responsible for the tragedy that had killed his brother?

There would be no more tragedies today. On that he was determined.

Uprooted palm trees were being swept along like matchsticks. Desert storms arrived fast, and subsided just as quickly, but the devastation they caused could have tragic, long-term consequences. Isla would be safe if she had stayed in the tent, but he doubted she would have gone there, as she had been so keen to finish her work. She was still here somewhere, he was sure of it— but where? She would have to climb to at least thirty or forty feet above the riverbed to be safe.

Looping a rope around a rock, he heaved himself up and climbed on, telling himself that she was sensible and resourceful. She had proved herself in the sandstorm, and he'd warned her not to go near the riverbed. She would be safe.

She had to be safe.

He'd climbed high enough to catch sight of the tent through the driving rain, and he scanned the area between there and the oasis.

There was no sign of Isla.

The water was crashing around one side of

the rocky outcrop, destroying everything in its wake, while on the other side the scenery was unchanged. He could only hope that Isla's smarts had kept her on the safe side of the cliff.

She was on a ledge, safe for the moment, with the gangly animal in her arms, resting before she pressed on, when a dark shape loomed over her.

'Shazim!'

She couldn't have been more surprised to see him climbing down to her, having come over from the other side of the cliff.

'Are you okay?' he asked, taking in the situation at a glance.

She nodded as his eyes blazed into hers. Without another word, he took the fawn and lifted it onto his shoulders. 'Come on. We can't stay here. The water's still rising.'

'No.' She shook her head as he held out his hand to help her. 'You need both hands to climb— it isn't safe. I won't be responsible for sending the ruler of Q'Aqabi plunging to his death.'

The change of expression on Shazim's face shocked her.

'Take my hand,' he repeated harshly. 'We have hardly any time left before the next wave of water sweeps us away.'

Ignoring him, she crabbed sideways until she found a foothold. Then, launching herself into space, she somehow landed on a narrow ledge. Once she was sure it cold hold her, she instructed, 'Pass me the gazelle.'

'No. You're not strong enough.'

'Pass him up,' she insisted.

He didn't doubt Isla's courage, but she didn't have the strength for this. The gazelle, meanwhile, made its own choice, and coiled around his neck in terror, refusing to move.

'Stay where you are,' he called out. 'I'm coming up.' Having found the entrance to a cave in the cliff face, Isla was taking refuge there. When he reached her she was ashen-faced. Carefully disentangling the gazelle, he set the small animal on the path to freedom. Dragging Isla into his arms, he embraced her with relief. As she clung to him he wondered if he could ever let her go. 'I'm sorry this had to happen. It's my fault for leaving you.'

He pressed his face into her hair, but she pulled back and shook her head. 'I knew what I was doing. I'm not a fool, Shazim.'

'No,' he argued grimly. 'You're anything but a fool, but you could still have been killed.'

'You left me for what you thought was a few short minutes,' she argued. 'If I can't cope in the desert for that long, then I don't belong here.'

'But if anything had happened to you—'

'It didn't. And if it had, *I* would have been responsible, not you.'

'You're wrong,' he said coldly. 'I would have been responsible, because I brought you here.'

'What's really wrong with you, Shazim?' she demanded. 'You don't come into the desert unless you can help it these days, your rangers told me. You set up one of the most important conservation programmes in the world, and then you stand back and let others take the glory, while you micromanage the scheme from a distance. The project only exists because of you—'

'You're so wrong about that,' he said bitterly.

Isla shook her head. 'It exists because of you, and not because some ghost from the past is directing you from afar. This is your project—your work—your triumph.'

'You don't know what you're talking about!'

'Don't I? I know what I see. You didn't bring me here to be a puling milksop who agrees with every word you say. You brought me here to challenge and question, and to add value to your scheme. And I will, if you'll allow me to. But if I can't be trusted alone in the desert, then I don't know where we go from here.'

'By bringing up the past, you are treading very dangerous ground,' he said icily.

'I wouldn't know, as you've never told me anything about your past. I only know what the rangers tell me—that everything you do here is to honour your brother's memory. But how are you honouring him if you can't trust the people you bring out here to help with the conservation programme? Is it because you don't trust yourself? Is that why you're behaving like this with me—as if I'm not capable of doing anything on my own?'

He made an impatient gesture. 'What's wrong here is that you don't listen to me.'

'Oh?' Hand on chest, she feigned surprise. 'And here's me thinking we would listen to each other.'

'You should have stayed away from the riverbed. You shouldn't have come here in the first place—'

'I shouldn't be here in the desert? Or I shouldn't be here in Q'Aqabi with you? Are you changing your mind about inviting your prize winner to visit your country, Shazim? Is that what this is about? You wanted to sleep with me, so you played along with that aspect of the prize, but now that you've had me I'm in the way. Maybe I'm even a potential embarrassment for you. Is that what you think?'

'This is not what this is about and you know it,' he said, growing equally heated.

'Do I? It seems to me that the ruler of Q'Aqabi gets everything he wants when he wants it, and when he's done with it he turns his back and rides away.'

'It was not like that.'

The shadows of the cave added menacing contours to the lines of Shazim's face, but she wasn't nearly done with him yet. 'What exactly was it like, Shazim? You brought me here to seduce me—and not just sexually. You got me to drop my guard—' Emotion got the better of her, and she made a brief angry gesture of frustration. 'You wooed me with words and with the magic of the desert. You listened to my fears, and plumbed my sorrows, without telling me a single word about yours. Did you feign interest just to get me into your bed?'

Shazim looked shocked and angry, but she couldn't stop now. 'Was this all a ploy to get what you wanted from me?' She gestured around. 'You took my trust and you abused it. You took my sorrow and made it your own—or you appeared to do so. Now I can only think you were getting me to open up and relax so you could get on with the job of seducing me. Have me, and then send me home. Job done. Well, I've got news for you, Shazim of Q'Aqabi. You're so used to people obeying your smallest whim, you can't see when they're doing something out of genuine concern for you. I admired you and everything you've done for Q'Aqabi, but now I feel sorry for you, because you'll never know what it is to risk your heart—'

'What's my heart got to do with this?'

He might as well have tipped a bucket of icy water over her head. Shazim couldn't have sounded more bemused.

'Exactly,' she said, raking her hair with frustration. 'You don't allow yourself to feel, so your heart has got absolutely nothing to do with this. Our relationship, as far as you're concerned, is purely that of employer and employee who undertook some pleasurable extramural activity. The fact that we slept together—and, I believed, became close—means nothing to you. I was on your agenda—on your schedule of things to do. And when you'd done me—done *with* me—you left for your next appointment,' she roared, all out of words.

CHAPTER SIXTEEN

'YOU'RE SO WRONG, ISLA. I don't know what you expect from me. I never promised you anything,' Shazim rapped with an angry gesture that took in his royal person, as well as her position as a vet on his team, together with the fact that at that moment they might have been talking two very different languages.

Isla gave a grim laugh. 'And you don't disappoint. Now,' she said as she walked to the mouth of the cave to look out, 'do you think we should try and get out of here? Because I do.'

Shazim's hand on her arm was meant to calm her, she was sure. 'I'm just glad you're safe,' he said.

She wanted to believe him and heaved a troubled breath.

'Your emotions are threadbare,' Shazim insisted. 'You need to calm down. If we're going to climb our way out of this cave safely, you need all your concentration.'

He was right about that, at least. 'I am calm—

well, at least I am now,' she said, frowning. 'And if my emotions are threadbare, it's because I care for you, you stubborn—'

'Me stubborn?' he said.

'Yes. You,' she insisted fiercely. 'The longer you nurse your wounds, the more they'll fester. Let me in, Shazim—if not me, then at least promise you'll let someone in.'

'Let you in?' he echoed, frowning. 'Do you think I have the luxury of emotion in my position?'

'You said that I'm a woman as well as a scientist. Doesn't the same rule apply to you? You're a man as well as a king, Shazim. You're allowed to feel.'

She gasped as he dragged her into his arms.

'And you torment me beyond reason—'

As Shazim growled something vicious in his own tongue he slammed his fists on either side of her face. Pinning her back against the smooth, cold stone, he thrust his powerful frame against hers, melting her anger with his passion, and turning her frustration into searing heat.

'Stop—stop it—' She pummelled his chest.

'If I thought for one moment you meant that—' Shazim stood back, removing all contact from her. 'Do you?' he demanded. His blazing stare burned into hers.

'No,' she admitted, just as angry as he was as she reached for him.

They came together forcefully, love and desire colliding, dissolving her will in her urgency to be one with him. From there it was a fast road to an inevitable conclusion. Shazim lifted her, and supported her with his hands clasping her buttocks, while she locked her legs around his waist. She was more than ready for him, and while she laced her fingers through his hair to keep him close, Shazim gave her what she needed in firm, deep strokes. Her entire body was one with his, but she was only aware of a mutual and desperate need to reinforce trust in each other. Shazim moved as fiercely as she did in the hunt for release, and when it came it was as powerful and as vital to both of their existence as the air they were so greedily gulping in.

When she calmed, and Shazim was still holding her, he murmured in between kissing her, 'We have to climb the cliff, *habibti*. You must save your strength for that.'

Humour coloured his dark, husky voice, but she wasn't done with him yet. Shazim was still hard, still lodged deep inside her. She rotated her hips, wanting more.

He was lost the instant she moved again. Dipping at the knees, he took her firm and deep, thrusting to a rhythm as old as time. He wanted this woman with a hunger that would not abate. He thought about her every waking moment. She kept him awake at night. He knew how to bring her to the edge and take her over, and he did so efficiently and fast. They did have to move on. There was no more time to lose.

'Now,' he instructed softly as she groaned with pleasure.

She broke apart in his arms, while he made sure that she enjoyed the very last wave of pleasure, and then he held her until she collapsed, spent in his arms.

'You're amazing,' she said softly.

'So are you.' He smiled against her mouth.

'What are we going to do about this, Shazim?'

'Do?' He lowered her to the ground. 'We've got to get out of here first.'

'That isn't an answer.' But then she removed her hands from his steadying grip as if she had come to a decision. 'But you're right,' she said. 'We should focus on climbing the cliff.'

Her voice sounded strained and had lost all the passion it had so recently held. Isla could always snap back into practical mode, but he knew she was hurting inside and he could offer her nothing. He followed her glance outside the cave to where the water was still roaring. 'Let's make a move.'

'Do you have enough rope?' she asked, checking what little equipment they had.

'It has to be enough.'

'Is it safe?' She stared at the coiled rope, chalk, and climbing gloves.

None of this was safe, but they had no choice. He wasn't sitting around to wait and see. Action was always his preferred option. 'The rope will take our weight easily. I've only got one pair of gloves, so you wear them—they'll protect your hands,' he insisted when she started to argue.

'Yes. Both of my hands in one of your gloves,' she remarked with a look. 'You wear the gloves. I'll take the chalk.'

He could see her now, heading up his team in the desert. Once Isla was fully conversant with all the dangers that team might face, she would make a formidable leader. But could he risk the life of someone like that to a perilous climb?

'I'd rather you stayed here and I bring the helicopter to lift you—'

'No,' she insisted. 'If you're going, I'm coming with you.'

'It's a hard climb, and too much of a risk.'

'That's for me to decide. Coming to Q'Aqabi was a risk, but I'm here. You risked a dangerous climb to come and find me. Are you saying I can't do the same?'

'You're not strong enough.'

'Inaction isn't an option for me, either, Shazim. Let's do this—'

He snatched the rope out of her hands. 'You're staying here.'

'What's really bugging you, Shazim? I know it's more than this or the storm—'

'I'm asking you to wait this out,' he spelled out as they faced each other angrily. 'What's so hard for you to understand?'

'You,' she retorted. 'You're impossible to understand.'

With an immense call on his patience, he tried sweet reason. 'It's much safer for you to wait until I come back with the helicopter rescue team. It will be easier—'

'Easy?' she queried. 'We're not here for easy, Shazim. If we liked easy, you would be on a yacht somewhere, living the playboy life with a supermodel on your arm, and I'd be in a nice, comfortable city practice with a regular wage and drinks down at the pub on a Friday night.'

As they stared grimly at each other, he knew she would never give up.

'Tell me,' she said. 'Tell me what's really bugging you.'

'If I do, you'll beg me to let you wait for the helicopter.'

'Try me,' she said.

Shazim was silent so long she wondered if he could hear the water creeping closer.

'My elder brother was killed saving me from a cliff like this,' he said at last.

She stilled, not wanting to distract him as Shazim stared blindly out of the cave at some horror she would never see.

'He overbalanced and slipped—'

When he didn't say anything more, she prompted him. 'Are you saying that you believe the fall was your fault?'

'It was my fault. He wouldn't have been anywhere near that cliff, if not for me.'

'But he was there and he saved you,' she argued pragmatically.

'I told him I could get down without his help. I was young and wild, and I believed I was indestructible. My brother was a lot older than me, but not nearly as strong. He was the thinker, while I was the reckless brother—'

'He liked to put plans together for the benefit of Q'Aqabi,' she guessed. 'Like the nature reserve,' she added as the pieces of the jigsaw fell into place. 'No one needed to tell me, Shazim,' she said when he stared at her. 'I've seen the way you devote your life to this project. I've seen your face when you discuss your ideas, and I know how far you'll go to advance them. This nature reserve is more than a passion for you, Shazim, it's your life's work.'

She understood him now. Nothing gave Shazim

respite from the guilt he felt about his brother's death. That was why he set himself such impossibly high standards and why he gave himself no rest.

'My brother was steady and cautious,' he said, shaking his head as if he still couldn't believe what had happened after all these years. 'He loved the desert he'd been born to rule, but he could never come to terms with its unpredictability. There had to be a rationale, a pattern to everything, he used to say, but the desert defied his best attempts to order it, and, in the end, I think that frightened him.'

She thought so too, and, remembering the theorising of the academics at her university, she knew now that there was nothing to beat knowledge combined with demanding and even very dangerous first-hand experience.

'He'd be proud of you, Shazim. You've turned your brother's dreams into reality.'

'But have I succeeded?' Shazim's fierce face was shaded with concern.

'That's why I'm here,' she said. 'You've not just succeeded, you've created a world-renowned facility that attracts a global audience. As far as I'm concerned, working here would be a dream come true.'

They both glanced out of the cave to see the

floodwater lashing at branches only a few yards away from them. They moved as one.

'Just one thing,' Isla said, staring at Shazim's outstretched hand. 'Before we leave here, I want you to accept that the past is the past for both of us. You can't go on blaming yourself for ever—'

'Leave it, Isla. I am to blame.' Shazim's expression blackened as he picked up the rope.

'You came to save me,' she pointed out, standing in front of him so she could meet his fierce stare levelly.

'That's different. I know what I'm doing. My brother should have left me on that ledge to freeze. *I* should have died instead of him—'

'No—' She grabbed hold of him when he collected up the rest of their equipment. 'Don't walk away from this, Shazim. Confront it.'

'What do you think I do every waking moment?' he demanded, swinging round.

'I think you rehash it—I think you replay it over and over to see if you could have done something differently—'

'I've told you all you need to know.'

His eyes were cold, his voice dismissive.

'You've told me the sanitised version,' Isla argued. 'Now tell me the rest.' His brother's death had overshadowed Shazim's life, and this perilous moment might be the only chance he ever got to start healing.

'What do you want to know?' He thrust his face into hers. 'Do you want to hear that my brother tried to save me and that he fell instead?'

'I want you to accept that you're not personally responsible for everything that goes wrong. I will never believe you caused your brother's death intentionally. You're innocent, Shazim. What happened was a tragic accident.'

His black eyes raked her face in fury. His balled fists were bleached with tension. Her heart went out to him, but she wouldn't relent. No one could live through that sort of torment without it destroying him in the end.

With a roar of impatience, Shazim rapped out, 'My brother took a chance to save me, as you risked your life to save that animal. Unlike you, he missed his footing. He held on for as long as he could, and I somehow managed to scramble down to him. I even found a good handhold, and reached out to take hold of his hand. He looked at me and smiled with such relief when I grabbed him, but I knew at once that I couldn't take his weight. He saw it in my eyes… There was such love in his eyes when he let go.'

There it was, laid out in front of her, pain of a type that few people, thank God, would ever know. She had often wondered if she would get over her mother's death, but she couldn't begin to imagine how Shazim must feel, believing himself responsible for what had happened to his brother.

'The nature reserve is your work, Shazim,' she told him gently. 'It's the most wonderful tribute to your brother. You've built a legacy in his name that will last for generations.'

Frowning bitterly, he shook his head. 'All that's left of my brother is the fountain I built in his honour, and my work in his name. Do you seriously think that can make up for his death?'

'No. Of course not.'

'You think I'm doing something admirable here?' His expression was derisive, self-hating, and riven with pain. 'Everything I do, everything I am, is thanks to him. He should be here now, not me.'

'And if he were here instead of you,' she argued, out of patience, out of time, Isla realised as she glanced outside the cave at the rapidly rising water, 'we'd probably die in this cave. I'm sorry to be so brutal, Shazim. I know you loved your brother, and I'm gutted that you lost him, but you can't spend the rest of your life blaming yourself for something you can't change. You're not a selfish youth now, you're a good man. Your brother wanted to prove how much he loved you by conquering his most deep-seated fears. He confronted the desert. He climbed a cliff. His only thought was to save you. He was a hero. At least allow him that.'

Her passionate words rang in the sudden silence and, for a moment, she wasn't sure how Shazim would respond. His expression was fixed and shocked, but to her relief it slowly changed into something more human and alive. It was the expression of someone who could feel. Emotion flashed behind his eyes, and then finally his shoulders relaxed.

'How long are we going to stand here?' she demanded then in her most practical tone. 'Shall we try for that ledge?' She glanced up to a path beyond the ledge that would take them to safety.

Shazim's silence was the longest few seconds of her life.

'Stand on my shoulders.' His voice rang out.

She did so.

He held onto her legs, keeping her steady. As soon as he was sure she was safely onto the ledge, he followed, and he kept on climbing until he reached a point where he could lean down and offer her his hand.

'Grab my wrist, Isla. I'll pull you up. Trust me…'

She didn't hesitate. Holding Shazim's stare, she took a firm grip of his wrist, and he hauled her up to safety.

CHAPTER SEVENTEEN

THE FIRST THING they did when they reached the safety of the tent was to call to reassure people they were safe. Within minutes of that, the sound of rotor blades approaching made talking impossible, and it wasn't until the engine had been turned off that Shazim was able to make himself heard.

'You're going straight back to the city for a thorough medical check-up.'

'That's not necessary,' Isla protested, suddenly suffused with dread at the thought of a second abrupt parting. They had opened their hearts to each other, Shazim had saved her life, and now he was returning to business as if nothing had happened?

'I say it is necessary for you to receive a full medical check-up,' he insisted without emotion. 'Your safety is of paramount importance to me.'

'Really?'

'Yes,' Shazim said grimly as a team from the

helicopter filed into the tent. Staring over her head, he issued a number of brief commands in Q'Aqabian, from which she gathered that she was to be escorted away.

'Excuse me just a moment,' she said in a loud, clear voice. 'I haven't finished talking to His Majesty.'

Shocked glances flew to her face. Everyone understood the gist of her appeal, and the fact that she had just disobeyed their Sheikh.

Shazim made a gesture to his men to give them space.

'Thank you,' she said. 'What we've been through was so intense, and now this seems to sudden.' She gestured at the helicopter. 'I just need you to reassure me that you won't go back inside your ivory tower—that you'll remember what we talked about on the cliff, and that you'll always believe—'

'We've said enough on that subject,' Shazim informed her, turning away.

'Have we? If we have, then, who will talk about your brother?'

His eyes when he swung back to look at her were murderous.

'I'm not frightened of you, Shazim, but I am frightened that you'll go back to avoiding the truth about your brother—about us—'

'Us?' he queried coldly. 'There is no us.'

'No,' Isla agreed sadly. 'I think you're probably right.'

There was nothing more to say. Shazim strode to the entrance of the tent to summon his men back in. He was right to end things between them. It was up to her to accept that what they'd enjoyed so briefly was over. Shazim had to return to his royal duties, and she had to return to her work. He was already busy exchanging information with his men. No doubt he'd want a progress report on the tribesmen's dispute, along with a whole host of other royal concerns. She could understand the urgency to catch up, but while Shazim could close off his feelings like that, she had no confidence in his recovery, which meant his mission to be the very best of kings might never be realised.

And that was no longer something for her to worry about, Isla accepted as members of the Sheikh of Q'Aqabi's black-clad team escorted her to the helicopter and saw her safely strapped in.

That was an end of it—of the two of them, she thought, blinking tears from her eyes as the helicopter lifted off and wheeled away. This empty feeling was on her for falling in love with a desert king. They would never work closely together now, as she had dreamed they would. Maybe she would never see him again, except maybe in passing at the university. Though, now that she'd pressed him to talk about his brother, would he even want to speak to her again? Isla doubted it. She had uncovered a pain far greater than anything she could have imagined, and Shazim had no one to share that pain with. She'd been selfish. In trying to help him, her amateur psychology had only succeeded in causing him more pain. And now she was leaving him to cope with that alone.

Isla's official time in Q'Aqabi had ended. It nearly broke her heart to leave the rangers in the desert, her friends in the village, and the animal programme she had so hoped to be a part of. Three weeks after she had returned from her hospital check-up, there was still no word from Shazim. Rumour said he'd gone on a retreat into the desert—without guards, without rangers. This was a first for him since his youth, though his people greeted it with rejoicing, as it spoke of Shazim's commitment to them. Isla was glad too, as it seemed to be a sign of the recovery she had feared he wouldn't make. Shazim had a lot of history to work through, and solitude and thought could hopefully help him heal, as he came to terms with the facts of his brother's death.

A smile broke through her sadness when Millie called to say goodbye to her. 'I'm just downstairs,' Millie explained. 'Can I come up?'

'Of course.' Isla couldn't think of anyone who could lift her heart more. Well, one person, but he had chosen not to be here, which was perhaps just as well. Her heart couldn't take much more battering.

She was still packing up her belongings, ready for the long flight back to London, when Millie knocked on the door. Closing her case, she wheeled it to the door. Her heart was full when she opened it to find Millie waiting outside. They hugged without words, but then Millie stood back.

'Come in,' Isla insisted.

'No. You'll be fine. I just wanted to see you—just wanted to reassure myself—'

'About what?' Isla frowned. 'Shall I call you when I finish packing? I'd like to say goodbye properly—'

Millie was staring down the corridor leading to Isla's suite of rooms. And now she saw why.

'Shazim,' she whispered.

Dressed down in jeans and a plain black shirt, Shazim was walking towards them in silence, Unsure as to why he was here, she backed into the room after acknowledging him with a polite dip of her head.

'Isla…'

Raising her chin, she stared into his eyes as Shazim followed her in. 'Yes.' She heard the door click quietly behind her as Millie left them.

'Can you forgive me?' Shazim asked straight out.

'Forgive you?'

'For being blind… For being thoughtless—'

'Shazim—' Taking hold of his hands in a firm grip, she stared steadily into his eyes. 'I didn't know what to think when you had me airlifted out and you stayed behind,' she said honestly. 'I just hoped that wherever you went, and whoever you were with, you would heal.'

'I am healed, because of you.'

Letting go of his hands, she shook her head and stood back. 'No one could heal that quickly. Not after what happened to you. There is no miracle cure for grief. There are only coping strategies, and time to heal a wound that cuts so deep. You have to face it every day, and you have to work towards healing it, as if it were a real physical wound.'

'Then, I've taken my first steps, thanks to you.'

Isla remained silent. She wouldn't take the credit for Shazim deciding that the time had come to face his demons. She was just glad that he had.

'And now you're here to say goodbye to me.' She nodded her head, as if trying to convince herself that she could accept this and leave Shazim and Q'Aqabi behind for good.

'You didn't think I'd let you go without coming to say goodbye, did you?'

'To be honest, I didn't know what to expect.'

Perhaps she should have been angry with him for sending her back to the city without a discussion, but Shazim had been fighting his own inner struggle. Her impulse even now was to comfort him, but instead she accepted reality, extended the handle on her suitcase, and turned for the door.

'You're not going to let her leave without saying something, are you?' Millie demanded the instant Isla had stepped outside the room.

She was surprised to find Millie still standing there. And even more surprised when Shazim said, 'Please forgive my sister. She always did speak her mind.'

'Your sister?' Whirling around, she stared at him, and then the pieces of the jigsaw rattled into place. Shazim had told her about the royal nursery, and how his brother had been like a father to the royal children. And now Shazim was the father of his country, and had taken over the role of father to his siblings. Of course, he'd chosen his sister to meet the prize winner at the airport. It made perfect sense. Millie was probably as invested in the nature reserve as Shazim. She had lost a brother too, and she would naturally want to honour his memory.

'I would like to hear what you've got to say,' Isla admitted.

'You must,' Millie insisted. Taking hold of Isla's hand, she drew her back into the room. 'We need you in Q'Aqabi. The project needs you. My brother needs you most of all—' Turning, Millie fired a fierce look at Shazim.

'Isla is her own woman,' he commented. 'She will do as she wants.'

'Then let's hope she wants to stay—though, heaven knows, you don't make it easy, brother.'

'I'll do anything I can to help you,' Isla said as she stared into Shazim's eyes.

'You'll need a job contract first. And a decent salary,' Millie added, directing this at Shazim. 'Isla would work here for nothing, but you can't allow that. She can't live on hot air.'

'I'm sure we can sort something out,' Shazim said with amusement. 'Would you give us a moment?' he asked his sister.

'Do you want the job?' he asked Isla as soon as they were alone.

'You know I want the job.' She held his dark stare steadily. 'There is nowhere else on earth I'd rather be, and no work I'd rather do. I'll even put up with you to do it—if you're sure you want me here.'

'The project needs you,' he said gruffly. 'You've got a job for life, if that's what you want.'

'But not as your mistress,' she stated firmly.

'Please—' Shazim's expression suggested that truly was the last thing on his mind.

Okay. She got that. She had already concluded she was hardly mistress material. 'Sorry. That was presumptuous of me, but I had to be sure.'

'At least I can always trust you to lay your cards on the table,' Shazim said drily. 'I wouldn't want you to change. The job I'm offering won't be easy. I want you to act as deputy leader for my project. You'll be a bit of a gofer for the current leader to begin with, but what the man in question knows about desert lore can't be taught. I want you to work closely with him, and learn as much as you can, with a view to taking joint responsibility eventually. I've witnessed your leadership skills, and I've had experience of your courage. I've also seen a great deal of common sense—'

'That man—the leader of the project. It's you, isn't it?'

The hint of a smile softened Shazim's hard face.

'So I haven't offended you?'

'Offended me?' He frowned.

'By speaking my mind?'

'That's one of the things I like best about you.

When you're in my position, very few people will speak their mind, for fear of losing royal favour. That's something that's never troubled you.'

She laughed. Even if Shazim only *liked* her, it would be enough if she could work here. It would have to be enough, Isla told herself firmly.

'I read the report from the hospital,' he said. 'I was relieved you were okay.'

'Everyone was very kind, and it appears that, apart from a few broken nails, I got off lightly.' *Unlike you*, she thought, remembering Shazim baring his soul to her on the cliff face. But if that had prompted him to take a pilgrimage into the desert to face up to the past, then everything had been worth it. 'Are you all right?'

'Of course.' Shazim brushed off her concern.

'Are you sure?' she pressed softly.

A muscle in his jaw worked as he admitted, 'I've never told anyone how I feel about the past before.'

'And you chose me. That means a lot to me, Shazim.'

Shazim dipped his head until their lips were just a tiny distance apart. Staring deep into her eyes, he kissed her so tenderly she felt tears pricking. If not completely healed, Shazim was mending. Talking about the past, and how the terrible events had made him feel, must have been a release for him, and for that she was glad.

'So, when do I start my new job?' she asked, staring up with naked love shining in her eyes.

'Right now—if you want to?'

'I can't think of anything I want more,' she exclaimed.

'Can't you?' Shazim murmured.

Her stare steadied on his. 'What do you get out of teasing me, Your Majesty?'

'The same thing you get out of winding me up, I imagine. But, I love you, so...' He shrugged. 'What can I do about it? I don't want to let you go. Will you stay with me?'

For the first time since that encounter on the building site, Shazim was asking—he wasn't instructing or commanding. The all-powerful Lion of the Desert, His Majesty the Sheikh of Q'Aqabi, was simply a man telling a woman that he loved her, and he was putting his heart on the line as he asked if she loved him too.

'I love you more than anything in this world,' Isla said honestly.

Shazim's words were a balm to her aching heart. He was fierce, but she loved his brand of fierce. His arms were strong and he was a natural protector, and, though she was strong, she needed him, more than she could ever express. She would never let him down. She would fight for him, as she had fought for everything else in her life. She would be strong for him, and for

Q'Aqabi. They'd be strong for each other. She was complete with him, and flawed without him. She was his, body and soul. She loved him with everything she had. Every moment apart was too long, while every moment with Shazim was perfect.

'I'm so sorry I left you,' he murmured.

'I was so worried about you,' she admitted. 'But you run a country, so I understood...sort of.'

Shazim laughed. 'Will you be so different when you're running my nature reserve?'

'I doubt it,' she confessed. 'We both get lost in our work.'

'But I want more than work from you,' Shazim said, turning serious as he held her in front of him. 'I want a life with you, Isla. I want children with you. And I want time with you in the desert so our children learn desert lore from both of us. Don't look so surprised,' Shazim added as he looped his arms around her waist. 'I want to marry you. I'm asking you to be my Queen. You can't possibly think that anyone else could match up to you, Isla Sinclair?'

She wanted to take it in, and to be deliriously happy. She wanted to shout out loud and perform a happy dance, but instead her frown deepened. 'I'm just not queen material.' All her concern was for Shazim, who seemed to her to be on the brink of making a terrible mistake.

'You are so wrong.' Shazim turned serious. 'My people respect you—I respect you. What better material for a queen could there be than you? But more important, I love you. No one else will ever come close to the way I feel about you.'

'I feel the same,' Isla admitted, her throat burning with emotion. 'I can't ask for anything more.'

'Really?' Shazim lifted one ebony brow. 'You disappoint me, Isla Sinclair.'

As Shazim was backing her towards the sofa, he was probably right.

'Wear no underwear in the future,' he instructed, caressing her and arousing her until she was so frantic to be one with him she could only agree. 'Let me,' Shazim suggested calmly as she yanked at her clothes, and only succeeded in tying herself in knots as she struggled to get them off.

'How can you be so calm?' she demanded with frustration.

'The end game is worth it?' Shazim suggested with a wicked smile as he lifted her in one arm and shucked her jeans and thong off with his free hand.

And then he thrust deep, claiming her as she claimed him. Fiercely.

It was a while before she could speak, and then it was only to urge him on. 'I love that,' she gasped as Shazim held her firmly in place while he buffeted her rhythmically against the wall.

'Something else we have in common,' he remarked, upping the tempo.

'I love that even more—'

'I would never have guessed,' he murmured.

She screamed as he brought her to the edge and held her there.

'Concentrate,' he instructed.

'Please,' she exclaimed in desperation, clinging to him as she panted out her need.

Shazim laughed as he tipped her over the edge. 'I'll never get enough of you, Isla—or of this.'

'Mmm…glad to hear it,' she managed somehow. 'But I still don't think I can be your Queen.'

'Why not?' Shazim demanded, holding her at arm's length so he could stare into her face.

'I'd be hopeless—just look at the facts: I'd never be ready in time, because I'd always have some clinic or other to finish. I'd be with the animals when you needed me most. I'd be covered in mud or worse, when I should be all dressed up for some important function—'

Shazim shook his head. 'There is an answer to all of that.'

'Is there?' she asked, wanting to believe him.

'Sure.' Shazim gave a smile. 'I'm going to keep you locked away in my harem.'

Isla dismissed this idea with a huff. 'You can try. And, no harem,' she added fiercely.

Shazim's smile broadened. 'Leave your fantasies behind for once and consider this. Has it never occurred to you that I love you so much I'm prepared to compromise where your work is concerned, as I ask you to compromise where my duty to Q'Aqabi is concerned?'

'A duty I hope to share one day.'

'You will,' he promised, slanting a smile.

'So, you really do love me?'

'I really do,' Shazim confirmed.

But it still didn't seem right to Isla. She wasn't beautiful. She wasn't tall and elegant like all those princesses and celebrities Shazim could choose from. And she certainly wasn't slim. She was stocky and capable, and far happier wearing rubber gloves ready to go deep, to do whatever was necessary for an animal, rather than flitting about in an evening gown. Could she really see herself in a regal robe and tiara, with her hair neatly brushed, and the right words for every occasion on the tip of her tongue?

'I'm such a klutz. I'd be hopeless at it,' she fretted out loud.

'You're just the kind of hands-on queen my country needs,' Shazim argued.

'But how about you, Shazim?' she asked with concern. 'What kind of queen do *you* need?'

'I was hoping you'd ask that question, because I need you—'

'Be serious. I'm not compliant enough to be your Queen. I wouldn't fall in step behind you— though I might stumble in your wake. And, if I do take that job—'

'Is there any doubt?'

'No,' she gasped, horrified just at the thought of turning it down. 'But I'll have no free time. You should pick one of those celebrity types—' Isla frowned as she thought about it. 'Or a royal princess...' Her eyes glazed over as she imagined what it might feel like to be that beautiful royal princess on the eve of marrying Shazim...

'Earth to Isla,' Shazim murmured, jolting her out of the daydream. Cupping her chin, he made her look at him. 'You have no idea how much I love you, do you?'

'You should found a dynasty,' she said, still distracted by thoughts of whom he should marry. 'You should marry one of those princesses, settle down and have children. Make your life easy, Shazim, and let me go.'

'What was it you once said about easy? I don't think either of us is happy taking that route, are we?' Shazim's lips pressed down as he shrugged. 'Though my life would certainly be easier if I let you go. But I'm afraid there's a problem with that too.'

'I'm good with problems,' Isla offered. 'Tell me and I'll try to sort it out for you.'

'Marriage with a princess?' Shazim's mouth tugged in a quick grimace. 'That's not a concept I'm comfortable with. I never will be.'

'But—'

It was no use trying to fight him off when Shazim pulled her into his arms.

'What are you doing?' she demanded, putting up a token fight.

'Explaining to you that your life is going to be with me. I'm not sure how yet, but we'll work it out—though I do need your agreement if we're to be married, and you haven't given me your answer yet. How else can you be my Queen?' he prompted. 'Well? Do you agree? What's your answer, Isla? Will you do me the honour of agreeing to become my wife—my Queen?'

As Shazim knelt in front of her Isla was speechless for a moment, but then she did what felt right and knelt too, so they were facing each other. Shazim kissed her mouth, her earlobe, and then her neck…

'What you said,' she managed when she could catch breath enough to speak. 'Do you really want my answer now?'

'I've already guessed your answer, but you can tell me again, if you want to.'

'Yes,' she exclaimed.

'Just as I thought,' he murmured, kissing her again, but this time deeply. 'You're easy to persuade.'

'Depends on what the problem is,' she countered on a shaking breath. 'And now, no more talking. I need you to concentrate.'

'Again?' Shazim murmured, laughing softly against her mouth.

'Oh, yes,' she confirmed. 'Always again...'

It was hard to believe how far she had come in her trust of men, but Shazim wasn't just any man, he was the love of her life, this man she had given her heart to. There were so many times when he had shown her why she should trust him, and though Shazim had battled through terrible issues of his own while they'd been together, he had never let her down. More than that, he had opened up her world to amazing possibilities, and had expanded her horizons in every way.

'How can this work?' she asked later when they were lying with their limbs comfortably entwined in Isla's bed at the palace.

'Let me see,' Shazim said as he moved over her. 'I'm sure if I try hard enough, I can work something out—'

'Stop!' Isla exploded into laughter as Shazim tormented her with kisses and all kinds of unmentionable things. 'All the answers can't be found in bed.'

'But most of the problems can be solved here,' Shazim countered. As he was nudging her legs apart with one hard-muscled thigh at the time, she was in no mood to argue. 'We'll have to dig deep, of course,' he added, 'if we are to find the answer to making this work...' As he was lifting her and positioning her so she was straddling him, it didn't seem the right time to disagree.

'Look at me when I'm talking to you,' Shazim commanded.

'Must I?' She threw her head back on a groan.

'Yes,' Shazim insisted. 'Now, ride me,' he murmured, encouraging her with his hands.

'I'm getting quite good at riding.' She threw him a mischievous smile.

'You certainly are,' he agreed.

And then he turned her beneath him, and Isla, still being aroused from the last time, was ready to fly again, and one firm thrust was all it took.

CHAPTER EIGHTEEEN

'I CAN'T BELIEVE what you've done for me, Shazim.' It was the eve of their wedding and Shazim had promised Isla a wedding gift that would exceed her wildest dreams, but never in all her fantasies could she have conjured up anything as incredible as this. He had recreated the university coffee shop in every tiny detail, but on the banks of a glittering oasis.

'I hope you like it.'

'As temporary structures go, it's pretty impressive,' she admitted, shaking her head.

Shazim laughed and tightened his arm around her shoulders. 'You can keep it as long as you want to—turn it into a refreshment stop for the rangers if you like, or dismantle it. It's entirely up to you, but I do think you should take a closer look at it before you decide to do anything too drastic with it.'

'I can't wait,' she admitted. 'But this is far too much…'

'Money can buy anything, but it can't buy happiness. Isn't that what they say? Nothing I do for you could ever be too much. And isn't it usual for a bride to enjoy a pre-wedding get-together with her friends?'

'My friends?'

Isla was astonished when she walked inside. Just about everyone she knew was sitting at a booth, or at one of the basic Formica tables. Shazim had faithfully recreated every detail, even down to her high-vis' jacket hanging on a hook by the door.

And… No!

'Charlie?'

Bounding up to her grumpy ex-boss, Isla threw her arms around him, and only when she pulled back did she get chance to realise that even Charlie was smiling today.

'Latte? Or your usual double macchiato with a caramel shot?'

'Chrissie!' Hearing the familiar voice, Isla whirled around to show Shazim with a smile how much she appreciated the thought he'd put into this fantastic wedding gift. 'I don't believe this!'

As the two girls hugged, Isla realised that it wouldn't have been a proper wedding without Chrissie to help her dress for the ceremony. 'I don't know how to thank you,' she said, shaking her head as she turned around to look at Shazim.

'Yes, you do,' he murmured so that only they could hear.

Isla's heart flipped at the thought of their wedding night as Shazim gave her one last look before leaving her with her friends. The next time she saw him would be at their wedding tomorrow.

Their wedding! Her marriage to the man she loved...the man she would always love.

It didn't get any better than that. She would have married Shazim if he had been one of the roaming Q'Aqabian tribesmen, with only his horse, his cooking utensils, his bedroll and a tent to his name, Isla thought as she watched Shazim spring onto the back of his stallion and ride away.

'So...how does it feel to be almost Queen?' Chrissie asked her, green eyes wide with wonder as she looked at Isla as if she had never seen her before.

Isla pulled a comic face. 'A bit like sitting my finals all over again.'

'Then, let's not talk about it,' Chrissie agreed. 'Shazim said my job is to distract you, so you don't get nervous about the wedding. So, I've got a great idea—let's talk about me.'

Isla collapsed into laughter. 'Great idea. There are so many people I want you to meet.'

'Hot men?' Chrissie asked hopefully.

'Surprise—she cuts to the chase,' Isla teased, rolling her eyes as she gazed heavenwards. 'As it happens, I've got some very hot men I want you to meet. Shazim's got a lot of friends coming over for the wedding, so you can take your pick. Just don't get too distracted, because I'm going to need your help more than ever when you dress me for the ceremony.'

'I still can't believe you're marrying the Sheikh of Q'Aqabi.'

'How do you think I feel?'

'Loved. At least, that's how you look.' Chrissie studied Isla's face. 'You're all glowing and bright-eyed…' She drew in a long breath. 'You're not…'

'Maybe.' Isla grinned and shrugged. 'We're certainly putting in all the effort required, but it's still far too early to tell.'

Chrissie's face lit up. Reaching across the table, she grabbed hold of Isla's hands. 'Congratulations! You're going to make a fabulous mother. You've had the best teacher, after all.'

Touched by her friend's sincerity, Isla felt tears smarting behind her eyes. 'Thank you,' she said softly. Her mother had been constantly in her mind since Shazim had asked her to marry him, and she was confident her mother would be with her, watching over her daughter every step of the way on the happiest day of Isla's life.

They were to marry in his palace, and his last task was to persuade Isla to wear his mother's jewels. His people would expect it. The golden casket was to be delivered to Isla's suite of rooms at the palace. This was the same casket that had been placed into Shazim's hands by his mother on the day she had begged him not to throw away his life because of his brother's death. She had told him that that would be no tribute at all, a sentiment he hadn't heard echoed until Isla had said exactly the same thing to him.

Lifting the lid, he stared into the glittering depths, and then grinned. He could just imagine Isla's reaction when she saw them. She was so understated, so dedicated to her work, he couldn't be entirely sure that his bride wouldn't rush to the wedding still dressed in scrubs and overshoes, fresh from the operating theatre.

Mounting up, he turned his stallion towards the palace where thousands were due to arrive to witness their wedding. The palace courtyard was so vast that Isla would ride to the ceremony in a horse-drawn carriage. The matched greys were being groomed even now. He would be waiting for her, mounted on his stallion as tradition demanded.

'Ready for a quick getaway if I change my mind,' he'd teased her.

'Fine. Just leave me to my work,' she had countered with a cheeky grin, which had obviously called for more physical pleasure in order to persuade her once and for all that he would be there.

There wasn't a chance he would change his mind about his wedding tomorrow. He would never find another bride like Isla if he searched the entire globe.

On the morning of her wedding Isla could not believe how her life had changed since that one rainy day on a building site in London. She had asked the women of the village to come to the palace to help her dress, and Shazim's sister, Millie, as well as Chrissie. With all their help, she hoped that she might feel—if not yet a queen, then almost a queen.

'You look beautiful,' Chrissie said as Isla studied her reflection in the mirror.

'I certainly look different,' Isla conceded, turning this way and that to watch the diamond coronet sparkle on her hair.

She couldn't believe the jewels Shazim had given her. There were glittering bracelets, countless rings, and the dainty diamond anklet she had decided to wear today, together with sparkling earrings and, of course, the royal coronet.

She would only have to wear them on state occasions, Shazim had promised—or maybe in bed with him, if she felt like it.

Better confine them to state occasions, Isla had

concluded as she'd handled the priceless jewels with reverence. In bed with Shazim was always such a hectic affair she couldn't risk the coronet bouncing across the floor.

He had also suggested she could wear them to work—to impress the animals. She'd known he was only trying to tease her into accepting the riches that came with the job of Queen, and she had lost no time in teasing him back. 'Better not. Can't risk losing them down the sluice—'

Of course she would honour his people by wearing the jewels, as Shazim had explained they had been in his family for generations. She thought about his ancestors as she put them on, and made a sacred pledge to devote herself to Q'Aqabi as they had.

'Let me fasten your dress,' Chrissie insisted. 'We're running out of time.'

Shazim had flown Isla to Rome in his jet for the design and fitting of her wedding dress. It was a dream of a dress in cobweb-fine lace over a close-fitting base of cool ivory silk. There was a long, floor-length veil, lightly embroidered with diamonds and pearls, that billowed out behind her for more than twenty feet, and her hair, having been polished to a honeyed sheen, had been left loose to cascade around her shoulders, because that was how Shazim liked to see it.

A mischievous smile touched her lips when she

remembered how he liked to fist a hank of it so
he could ease her head back and kiss her throat—

'Isla?' Chrissie chivvied.

She stared at Chrissie blankly for a moment.
She had been so wrapped up in her fantasy—
a fantasy that, quite incredibly, was about to
become reality—that she hadn't heard a word
Chrissie had said.

'They're ready for you,' Chrissie prompted
gently, standing back.

'Your carriage awaits,' Millie added, leaning
forward to kiss Isla fondly on both cheeks. 'Welcome to the family, Isla.'

Millie was in charge of the wedding bouquet
that Shazim had had specially flown in, along
with all the wedding flowers, from the English
Channel Islands. The blush-pink, cream, and
ice-white roses had been chilled to keep them
fresh, and as Isla brought them to her face to
inhale their delicate scent she brushed the tips
of the petals against her cheek. They were cool
and slightly damp, and she knew at once what
she wanted to do with them, and she always followed her heart.

Shazim was waiting for her, mounted on his
stallion beneath a flower-strewn arch. Nerves
gripped her when she first heard the roar of the
crowd. There were so many people. As her carriage drew closer they seemed to form an endless

sea. She would have preferred a quiet, intimate ceremony, but had always known what she was getting herself into. This wasn't just her day, it was for the people of Q'Aqabi too, and that was a small sacrifice to put her wishes aside for them and for Shazim.

Shazim's smile was all the reassurance she needed, and as he helped her down from the carriage his expression was so intense and so loving that her world shrank around him, and she saw only him.

Shazim had never looked more astonishingly handsome. Dark and swarthy with his *howlis* covering his head, but not his face this time, he was dressed in black flowing robes, edged in gold. She had heard it said that brides went through their wedding ceremony in a dream, but she'd done with dreaming. Every single atom in her being was fully aware of the reality she was entering into. When she accepted Shazim's ring, she was accepting him as well as everything he represented. She was pledging to support him and his country, to share his life and his duty to the land he loved, and she couldn't have been more sincere when she made her vows.

'Do you like it?' he murmured as he placed the ring on her finger.

She would have loved anything Shazim had chosen for her, with the exception, perhaps, of that safety gear back at the building site. But this platinum band studded with diamonds was nothing short of spectacular. Like the man at her side, she thought, smiling up at him as the ceremony concluded and they were declared man and wife.

They walked through the crowd to their reception at the palace, and were cheered every step of the way. But there was just one small detour she wanted to make...

'What is it?' Shazim asked with concern when she touched his arm.

'There's somewhere I have to go.'

'Anywhere you want,' he said.

Linking arms with him, she walked up to the beautiful fountain Shazim had built in his brother's honour and, kneeling in front of it, she laid her bouquet down.

'For your brother, for your country, and for us,' she said, when Shazim raised her to her feet. 'But most of all, for you,' she whispered.

'How did I get to be so lucky?' he demanded, folding her arm through his.

'You found a high-vis' jacket that would fit me?' she suggested.

'I think it was a little more than that,' Shazim argued softly. 'I love you more than life itself, my beautiful wife.'

'I love you too,' she said with belief in the very brightest of futures shining in her eyes.

EPILOGUE

TICKLE TORTURE WENT on for much longer that night. No wonder the children refused to go to bed when Shazim got them so excited. And it was the same each night, just when she got them calmed down. But when he looked at her and shrugged with that look in his eyes, she would forgive him anything. He was the most wonderful father to their three children, and the most wonderful man to share her life with. He hadn't stopped at recreating the café in London to make her happy. Sensing something of her feelings on living such a public life, he had built them a getaway on the outskirts of the city, where they could enjoy a proper family life. This wasn't just any getaway, but a building he had designed to remind her of the simple cottage where she had lived as a child.

Though Shazim's version of the cottage was at least twice as big, she had to tell him tactfully, and the home she'd grown up in hadn't been packed to the brim with Shazim-style luxuries. But that was one of the benefits of marrying not just a king, but a highly skilled architect who was always creating the most innovative structures. Her children had been born here, and the kitchen was her own—such a small thing, but it meant the world to her, and to their daughter, Yasmin, who was rapidly turning the kitchen into a makeshift clinic for the overflow of pets, having recruited their twins, Darrak and Jonah, to act as her rangers.

'Bed,' Isla insisted firmly. The children reluctantly obeyed her command. They had already learned that Daddy might be King, but ignore Mummy at your peril.

'Can I come to the clinic with you tomorrow?' Yasmin begged, clinging to Isla's hand while her brothers jumped up and down in an attempt to catch their share of Isla's attention.

Isla's clinic was thriving and, with Shazim's help, she had opened three more. She was still happiest dressed down in work clothes, she reflected wryly as she hugged and kissed her children before they went to bed, but she had learned to act like a queen and to wear the beautiful jewels that Shazim's mother had left him with such love and pride, as she should, to honour the memory of a woman who had known such immense love, as well as such terrible grief.

'If you go to bed now, and I don't hear another sound out of you until the morning, you can *all* come to the clinic with me.'

Luckily, Shazim swept all three of them up, or their shrieks of excitement might have deafened her, Isla decided, laughing as she went to help to tuck them in.

When it was all quiet upstairs, Shazim came to stand with her on the beautiful veranda overlooking the oasis. As he linked his arms around her waist, she nestled back against the man she loved and smiled. They were so close in heart and spirit that, even with her back to him, Shazim could feel the change in her. 'No,' he said in wonder.

'Yes,' she softly replied.

'I think we should go to bed to celebrate the arrival of another child.'

Turning, she smiled into the eyes of the man she loved, and trusted with her life, and all her heart. 'I thought you'd never suggest it…'

* * * * *

If you enjoyed this story, check out these other great reads from Susan Stephens:

BOUND TO THE TUSCAN BILLIONAIRE
BACK IN THE BRAZILIAN'S BED
BRAZILIAN'S NINE MONTHS' NOTICE
AT THE BRAZILIAN'S COMMAND
IN THE BRAZILIAN'S DEBT

Available now!

LARGER-PRINT BOOKS!
GET 2 FREE LARGER-PRINT NOVELS PLUS
2 FREE GIFTS!

HARLEQUIN®

Romance

From the Heart, For the Heart

LARGER-PRINT BOOKS!
GET 2 FREE LARGER-PRINT NOVELS PLUS
2 FREE GIFTS!

HARLEQUIN

super romance

More Story...More Romance

LARGER-PRINT BOOKS!
GET 2 FREE LARGER-PRINT NOVELS PLUS
2 FREE GIFTS!

H HARLEQUIN®

INTRIGUE
BREATHTAKING ROMANTIC SUSPENSE

YES! Please send me 2 FREE LARGER-PRINT Harlequin® Intrigue novels and my 2 FREE gifts (gifts are worth about $10). After receiving them, if I don't wish to receive any more books, I can return the shipping statement marked "cancel." If I don't cancel, I will receive 6 brand-new novels every month and be billed just $5.49 per book in the U.S. or $6.24 per book in Canada. That's a saving of at least 11% off the cover price! It's quite a bargain! Shipping and handling is just 50¢ per book in the U.S. and 75¢ per book in Canada.* I understand that accepting the 2 free books and gifts places me under no obligation to buy anything. I can always return a shipment and cancel at any time. Even if I never buy another book, the two free books and gifts are mine to keep forever.

199/399 HDN GHWN

Name _____ (PLEASE PRINT) _____

Address _____ Apt. # _____

City _____ State/Prov. _____ Zip/Postal Code _____

Signature (if under 18, a parent or guardian must sign) _____

Mail to the Reader Service:
IN U.S.A.: P.O. Box 1867, Buffalo, NY 14240-1867
IN CANADA: P.O. Box 609, Fort Erie, Ontario L2A 5X3

**Are you a subscriber to Harlequin® Intrigue books
and want to receive the larger-print edition?
Call 1-800-873-8635 today or visit www.ReaderService.com.**

* Terms and prices subject to change without notice. Prices do not include applicable taxes. Sales tax applicable in N.Y. Canadian residents will be charged applicable taxes. Offer not valid in Quebec. This offer is limited to one order per household. Not valid for current subscribers to Harlequin Intrigue Larger-Print books. All orders subject to credit approval. Credit or debit balances in a customer's account(s) may be offset by any other outstanding balance owed by or to the customer. Please allow 4 to 6 weeks for delivery. Offer available while quantities last.

Your Privacy—The Reader Service is committed to protecting your privacy. Our Privacy Policy is available online at www.ReaderService.com or upon request from the Reader Service.

We make a portion of our mailing list available to reputable third parties that offer products we believe may interest you. If you prefer that we not exchange your name with third parties, or if you wish to clarify or modify your communication preferences, please visit us at www.ReaderService.com/consumerschoice or write to us at Reader Service Preference Service, P.O. Box 9062, Buffalo, NY 14240-9062. Include your complete name and address.

HILP15

WESTERN (WP) PROMISES

YES! Please send me **The Western Promises Collection** in Larger Print. This collection begins with 3 FREE books and 2 FREE gifts (gifts valued at approx. $14.00 retail) in the first shipment, along with the other first 4 books from the collection! If I do not cancel, I will receive 8 monthly shipments until I have the entire 51-book Western Promises collection. I will receive 2 or 3 FREE books in each shipment and I will pay just $4.99 US/ $5.89 CDN for each of the other four books in each shipment, plus $2.99 for shipping and handling per shipment. *If I decide to keep the entire collection, I'll have paid for only 32 books, because 19 books are FREE! I understand that accepting the 3 free books and gifts places me under no obligation to buy anything. I can always return a shipment and cancel at any time. My free books and gifts are mine to keep no matter what I decide.

272 HCN 3070 472 HCN 3070

Name _____ (PLEASE PRINT) _____

Address _____ Apt. # _____

City _____ State/Prov. _____ Zip/Postal Code _____

Signature (if under 18, a parent or guardian must sign) _____

Mail to the **Reader Service**:

IN U.S.A.: P.O. Box 1867, Buffalo, NY 14240-1867
IN CANADA: P.O. Box 609, Fort Erie, Ontario L2A 5X3

* Terms and prices subject to change without notice. Prices do not include applicable taxes. Sales tax applicable in N.Y. Canadian residents will be charged applicable taxes. This offer is limited to one order per household. All orders subject to approval. Credit or debit balances in a customer's account(s) may be offset by any other outstanding balance owed by or to the customer. Please allow 4 to 6 weeks for delivery. Offer available while quantities last. Offer not available to Quebec residents.